THE TEXAN
FROM MONTANA

Al Cody

WITHDRAWN
COST:

Curley Publishing, Inc.
South Yarmouth, Ma.

Library of Congress Cataloging-in-Publication Data

Cody, Al, 1899–
    The Texan from Montana / Al Cody.
        p. cm.
    1. Large type books.   I. Title.
    [PS3519.O712T44   1990]
    813′.54—dc20
    ISBN 0–7927–0527–0 (lg. print)   90–32036
    ISBN 0–7927–0528–9 (pbk.: lg. print)   CIP

Copyright © 1970 by Lenox Hill Press

All rights reserved. No part of this book may be used or reproduced in any manner without written permission except in the case of brief quotations embodied in critical articles and reviews.

Published in Large Print by arrangement with Donald MacCampbell, Inc. in the United States, Canada, the U.K. and British Commonwealth.

Distributed in Great Britain, Ireland and the Commonwealth by CHIVERS LIBRARY SERVICES LIMITED, Bath BA1 3HB, England.

ESSEX COUNTY LIBRARY

Printed in Great Britain

FM92545

1

It was a good country to have behind rather
than lying ahead, waiting to be crossed – that
haunt of lost and lawless men which some
called The Nations. It was big and wide,
starkly impressive, at times beautiful. Gila
monsters and diamondback rattlers also had
elements of stark beauty, but all three were
savage and untouchable.

Now The Nations were behind, and Texas
was ahead. It was homecoming, in a sense,
after the long, bitter years of war. Lee had
surrendered.

The warm scents of spring, of earthy,
growing things, were pungent in the
nostrils. Here, where only the backwash
of war had touched, was a deceptive air
of peace and security, golden with promise.
Jogging bareback astride a big mouse-colored
mule, Montana Abbott resisted the impulse
to kick his steed into a run. It was better to
cover the miles at a steady pace, but to keep a
reserve of speed and energy against the need of
possible emergencies.

Fate had its odd quirks, like dark laughter.
Two letters had reached him on the same day,

1

delivered at Bozeman, Territory of Montana. One had been his discharge from the Union army, making him his own man again after the long years of war. It meant release, a chance to search and explore, perhaps to find a fortune in the gold camps. . . .

Such thoughts had been in his mind, but the second letter was a checkmate. It had been a long time on its way, usually weeks or months behind him, finally catching up – the first word from home in more than two years.

The news it contained was grim, though not unexpected. There had been a lung fever in part of Texas during the late summer and fall of '63. Lung fever was as good a name as any for the ravage of epidemics. Both his father and mother had succumbed.

His brother Tom had survived the scourge, but now he was no more than half a man. Writing the news Tom had said he hoped that Bill would live to return to the ranch on the San Saba. What he did not say was starkly implied between the lines. The once prosperous ranch was on the verge of bankruptcy, cattle-poor – as was all of Texas.

Wasting no time, he had set out, taking the long trail south. The home ranch was not for him, nor would it ever be. He had been named William Montana Abbott, and now he was known as Montana, which to him was both satisfying and fitting. He belonged to Montana and in it; it had become his country.

But he owed it to Tom to pay him a visit, to help him if he could. That came first.

One emergency had arisen suddenly, amid a leafy meadow, some days before. Trouble was there, and he'd ridden straight into it.

That he might avoid it had occurred to him, but only as a passing thought. Experience had taught him that playing at being a Good Samaritan was usually a thankless job and a dangerous one. But men and women were there, under attack by a scurvy crew who could be designated as outlaws or renegades if one were prone to understatement. The presence of women in such a situation was reason enough for him to act, and to cap it he'd heard the frightened wail of a child –

A folly even bigger than his must have led the train of three wagons into such inhospitable country. Even a modicum of good sense indicated that at least ten times three should band together for reasonable safety. But there they were, three wagons only and under siege, and it was too late for other considerations.

The element of surprise sometimes played a big part, as he had learned as an officer of cavalry. Here he was only one man, but at least he was a big one – and not expected. He charged into the fray with a wild rebel yell,

3

giving the impression there were at least half a dozen men with blasting guns.

He hadn't done too badly. Before the outlaws understood, they had panicked and retreated, and the trio of wagons had succeeded in getting under way, through a narrow neck between the hills where the odds had been heavily against them. The last he'd seen, all of them with their occupants, had been at a wild run, vanishing in the distance.

Some of the startled attackers had rallied, and it had been hot work while it lasted. He'd found himself unhorsed, forced to fight on foot, his revolver empty, swinging a clubbed rifle. Before that terrible flailing the remnant had scattered, but only in the nick of time. He'd stumbled and gone down from a clout to the skull which brought night in the middle of the day even as they broke. . . .

By the time he was able to shake off the dizziness and get unsteadily to his feet, he was alone. The horse with which he'd set out from Montana was gone, strayed or stolen. The clubbed rifle was broken, useless.

Partly by way of compensation, he'd come upon the mule, standing motionless, big ears tipped forward, sheltered by a clump of trees and brush. He guessed that it had been with the wagons, breaking loose during the attack, sagaciously keeping out of sight.

4

Now he rode tall, showing a soldierly carriage despite the lack of a saddle and the weariness brought about by an endless trail. The gaunt look induced by years of war was gradually being replaced by a taut but healthy leanness, and his mustache above a clean-shaven face had a rakish tilt. There was a whimsical set to his mouth, an easy swing to his broad shoulders.

He was getting deep into Texas. Spring had exhibited its usual capriciousness as he journeyed, blowing hot one moment, rawly cold the next. But here, along the middle reaches of the San Saba, it seemed to have made up its mind, nestling snugly in the hollows, where the full green of spring lay tossed like a rumpled blanket. In the smiling sun was the promise of summer. The aches and stiffness of the cold years of war seemed lifted from his bones.

He was returning to Texas with almost the same worldly goods as when he'd left – the clothes on his back, a mule instead of a horse between his legs. Remembered landmarks brought an unexpected lump to his throat. Home lay just over the hill.

He flinched at the sound of guns booming in the distance. Guns were an old story, but these were different. Texas was vast and stuffed with potential wealth, but like most of the South, it lay prostrate, gripped by poverty. Overrun with vast herds of cattle for which there was no market, peace – or the end of war – had brought what some called opportunity, others a plague.

Hides could be sold to Gulfport packing houses or traded for lumber, for other desperately needed goods from the South, perhaps even from the North. So men were shooting cattle, killing them for their hides.

To Montana that seemed a dreadful waste, almost wanton slaughter. Cattle were meat as well as skin. But to get them to a market where the meat would bring a market price was so hazardous as to be counted impossible.

Water made a glint in the sun, a small stream crowding close beside the road. Wildcat Run. Many a time he'd fished it as a boy, wandering barefoot.

The mule turned and dipped its nose gratefully into a pool, and Montana swung down, easing the stiffness of outthrust legs about the barrel of the mule, strongly aware of the sweat and grime. He drank at a spot upstream, then frowned down at the reflection in the clear waters. Somehow, thinking back to the boy who had ridden away long years before with high hopes and the thrill of adventure, he felt as if he were meeting a stranger.

6

The crisp mustache was reddish and with a jaunty curl, in contrast to the black hair above, in which hints of frost mocked the memory of the boy. The eyes could warm to match the sky, but that was the only similarity to the youthful eyes. The hope had mostly washed away, leaving them with the calculation of a man who had companioned too long and often with death. The lines of the mouth, tight-set below the mustache, suggested a quality of relentlessness unknown to the boy.

Half a decade had produced changes, but he was one of the lucky ones. At least he had survived, and to the outward glance he was sound of wind and limb. A saber scar was hidden by his shirt, and its sharp slash had missed his heart, though by a scanter margin than either he or his opponent had planned. A minie ball had passed through the muscles of his upper left arm, again missing his heart by inches, but the arm, aside from recurrent aches on cold nights, was as strong if not as supple as before. A bayonet thrust had left him with only a slight limp, noticeable at day's end when he was overly tired.

He climbed back, and the mule began its patient plodding, topping the rise, halting of its own accord. Montana eased a deeper breath into his lungs. There it was, much as

7

he remembered it – the long, sprawling 'dobe between great trees, thick-walled, massively unlovely, yet with a beauty of its own. The big log barn below, the weathered poles of the corrals and the outbuildings stood intact. Even a twist of smoke rose from the kitchen chimney.

The outbuildings were nearly a mile away, but Montana's eyes were keen. Sharp vision was more important than a rifle in a hostile community. A man came from the house, looking around, almost as though he had heard or scented the approach of an enemy. He could hardly have divined Montana's return, but the listening attitude, of wolf-like wariness, was not to be mistaken. Nor was the face below the big Texas hat, heavy-jowled, beard-stubbled.

"Watson," Montana murmured. "Jabez Watson – on Abbott land. What the devil is he doing there?"

Speak of the devil! In Watson's case, it was appropriate.

The Watsons had been neighbors of the Abbotts for as long as Montana could remember. Their spread encompassed most of the drainage of Stowaway Creek. They were Texans, and by that token Southerners, but all that was simply a result of geography. The Watsons had given neither loyalty nor service to either the Union or the Confederacy, but solely to the furthering of their own interests.

There had been antagonism and occasionally bad blood between the Watsons and the Abbotts for as long as the rival outfits had crouched along the reaches of the San Saba; but during those years, the Watsons had learned to respect the Abbotts.

What had occurred since Tom had written that letter, that a Watson was now on this spread, acting as though he owned it?

Watson turned back into the house, but reappeared almost at once, and several men came up from the barn at his call. They secured horses, then headed along the road toward where Montana waited. It was hardly possible that Watson could know anything of his return, though it almost seemed as if that were the case. But he was clearly giving the orders.

Pulling his mule behind a screen of trees and brush, Montana watched as the riders came up, then went on past. There were nine, armed and well mounted. Five rode horses with the Flying W brand on their right hips. The others were on cayuses with the A Bar on their right shoulders. All seemed to be from one outfit.

It might be better to ascertain what the

9

existing situation was before riding the rest of the way, or barging in with the questions or demands. A few more hours, after so many years, was not likely to make much difference. But whatever the situation, Montana doubted that Watson would welcome him with much cordiality.

The years had taught him, if not patience, at least the control of impatience. Montana headed away from the road to a half-wild, secluded glen. Here the years had made no change. He picketed the mule, then with hook and line snagged fish from the nearby run. Roasting fish or game had become a ritual of the trail. He ate in the last glow of sunset, then prepared for a few hours of sleep. Once the others were asleep as well, he'd go on for a better look.

He roused at a warning instinct, starting to sit up, to throw back his blanket, but the motion was a second tardy. Something was upon him, silent but savage, beating him down into a blackness darker than the surrounding night, into a pain-shot nightmare where the gloom was complete.

Montana's head throbbed as though the regimental drummer were beating a tattoo on his skull. He lay for a while, wondering confusedly if he was back on a battle-field. But there were no other wracked bodies as he pried open his eyes; only the clear dawn. Memory returned painfully.

The big mouse-colored mule was gone. The sun, slanting sharply against the ache of his head, was driving away the dew, though he was shivering. The reason for that was all too apparent. The rumpled blanket no longer covered him. He was in his long ragged underwear and nothing else. His somewhat frayed and worn clothing of the trail was gone, stripped from him while he was unconscious.

A hand to his skull explained the ache as well as the robbery, disclosing a sizable lump and a smear of dried blood. He had been slugged as he struggled to awake.

There were other factors which surprised him. As though left in exchange for his own clothes, a uniform had been tossed, in apparent haste, onto the ground. It was a captain's uniform, such as he had worn through the first years of the war – a Confederate uniform. In contrast with his own clothing, these garments were nearly new, in fairly good shape. There was a hat nearby to complete the outfit.

Montana examined them disbelievingly. Along with the uniform was a pair of revolvers. Colt's forty-fives. Nor were these ordinary weapons. They were long-barreled, and the handles were of pearl, gold-mounted and fancily embellished.

2

Shivering, Montana reached for the discarded uniform and pulled it on, and was not much surprised to find that the outfit fitted him as well as his own had done. The matter of size would have been taken into account by whoever had traded with him so unceremoniously.

Intrigued, he studied the new outfit. The trousers were of regulation bluish-gray, with a gold stripe running up and down. The coat had a broad belt; the sleeves were elaborate with braid. It was fancier than his own had been, more elaborate than the Union blue which he'd worn in the last months of the war, on a fighting rescue mission against the Indians west of the big river.

Under the coat, as though carelessly stripped off, was a cap and a pair of leather gloves. Such uniforms had been fairly common during the early days of the struggle, but had become increasingly rare, as hardship and poverty, together with a lack

12

of goods, compelled even officers to make do with whatever they could come by. Uniforms had often been a weird combination of Yankee and Confederate, in all sizes and designs.

To find such a uniform here, after the war had ended, was doubly strange, though no more so than the fancy guns. They were loaded, well oiled, in excellent condition. Thrown back in the brush, not quite out of sight, was an officer's artillery belt and holsters for the guns. These, by contrast, appeared plain and worn.

There must have been some compelling reason to cause the wearer to attack him and make the trade under such circumstances, especially to discard so fine a brace of guns. Probably it was because they would be as distinctively recognizable as the uniform. But at least these clothes were warm, in better condition than his own had been after the long journey down from Montana, and for him it was not a matter of choice.

Thrusting his hands into the pockets, he went taut with surprise. This grew to amazed disbelief as he brought the pair of coins into the light. Fingering them, he'd expected silver or copper at the most, but these were gold, each a double-eagle. They jingled pleasantly, and a close look assured him of their genuineness.

He eyed them with increasing wariness. Such hard money would scarcely have been left behind as an oversight. They suggested that the owner of the uniform had not been troubled, like the majority of the defeated army, by any lack of funds. In certain respects, the transaction added up more nearly to a trade than a robbery.

At that, it's no more than my mule was worth, Montana decided. And the money, like the fancy guns and the uniform, might be a trap, making him a marked man. He'd looked for trouble from Watson, but it had come from a totally unexpected source.

He'd better move warily, but move he must. His return to the ranch must be delayed. He'd head instead for Willow Run, the sleepy town of his boyhood days. Yesterday he'd by-passed the town, preferring to arrive at the ranch unannounced. Today there was a difference.

Exercise proved good for his headache, the throbbing gradually subsiding as he swung along, keeping well back from the road. Despite what he had seen at the ranch buildings the day before, the mystery of the night attack and the evidences of hardship which gripped the land, he knew a pleasurable excitement. Once more he was on familiar ground, country where he'd walked and ridden a thousand times. The easy roll of hills, the run of water, sweep of field and meadow were unchanged. So were the herds of cattle, grazing in the distance.

This had been cattle country for as long as he could remember, and now it was even more so. The range had become endangered by overgrazing. Though people had felt the impact of war, Texas cattle had never had it so good. Markets had dried up, blown away by the smoke of battle. Herds which had been pretty well domesticated had been left to run as they pleased, reverting in a few generations almost to the wild.

Montana moved behind a screen of brush or through gulches. A man on horseback was safe enough, but on foot he'd attract their interest, and with it, a lively curiosity which might change to hostility. Wild longhorns might run from a man, but they might just as readily run at him, to gore and trample him.

Something moved in the brush. Montana swung, looked, then approached with caution. His big mule nodded as though in greeting, waggling long ears. The bridle bit was in its mouth, the reins dragging.

Not far beyond, face down in the grass, he found the dead man. Almost concealed by intervening brush, the body was stiff to the touch, a sure indication that he'd not lived long after their prior meeting. From the way he huddled, oddly clumped, Montana deduced that he'd tumbled from the mule after being shot in the back. The wound tended to confirm that assumption.

As Montana had expected, he was about Montana's size and build, and he wore Montana's old clothes.

"But making the change didn't do you any good," Montana murmured. "Whoever was after you knew you anyhow – and bushwhacked you, as you knew they intended to."

Here perhaps was poetic justice, but the near-certainty that the rifle bullet might have found a target in his own back but for chance or mischance was not pleasant. No matter how often a man looked upon death, it was always grisly.

Apparently the killer had been satisfied with the results of his shot, not approaching to disturb the body or steal the mule. Montana turned the dead man so that he could see the face, but it brought no recognition. There was a superficial resemblance to his own, but it was not close enough to be striking.

Methodically he made an examination. There were no papers, nothing which furnished any clue to the dead man's identity. But in one of the pockets he found several more gold pieces.

Pondering, Montana took them. In normal times, such a death should be reported to the authorities. But these times were far from average, also, he doubted if there would be any proper officials to whom a report might be made. Doing so would not help the dead man, and it might put more hindrances in the way of his own homecoming.

He solved the dilemma to his own satisfaction, carrying the body to the bank of Wildcat Run, where high water, probably a flash flood, had undercut the nearer bank. Tucking the dead man back into the shady recess, he jumped on the shaky soil, above, caving it down. It was an adequate grave, better than many an honest soldier had received after the sweep of battle across a field.

"Rest in peace, friend," he adjured softly. "Perhaps I'll learn something more one of these days, maybe even find a way to take action – not that it makes much difference to you now, I guess."

It was pleasant to be astride his mule again, as he had long since acquired an aversion to walking. Boy and man, he'd pretty much lived on a horse's back, and the armies, appreciating his skill, had each assigned him to the cavalry. He was not out of place, clad again in the uniform of a captain of cavalry.

Willow Run appeared to have slumbered through the years of strife, unchanged and uncaring. Montana tied his mule to a chewed hitching rail and eyed the only restaurant hungrily. Its paint had been weathered to a ghostly grayness, but it seemed still in business, except that it lacked more than an hour of noon. So he crossed instead through soft dust to the barbershop; the dim interior was pleasant after the bright sun of the street.

Old Zeb Porter rose wheezily from his bench by the window and took up his shears. There was no recognition in his glance, though he addressed the uniform politely.

"You want a ha'cut, Cap'n, or mebby more?" he inquired, still without any show of interest.

"Haircut and shave," Montana instructed, settling himself in the chair. His whiskers had gone several days untended. "Leave my mustache and sideburns."

It was pleasant to relax, while Zeb worked and the long accumulation of hair grown on the trail littered the floor. A fly buzzed, skimming near the ceiling, and the increasing heat of midday crowded the room. Finally Zeb held a small mirror so he could inspect himself, and he regarded his smooth face with

18

mild pleasure. Zeb stared, and equal surprise and pleasure spread over his own face.

"Why, why – bless my soul and bootlaces, if it ain't Bill Abbott!" he exclaimed. "Just at first there I didn't know you, not with you grown to a man and an officer and all. You're back, boy – and a captain to boot! Well, for everlasting! Welcome back, Cap'n Abbott!"

Knowing Zeb as he did, Montana wondered how much of the warmth of that greeting was occasioned by the officer's uniform, and how much by himself. Not that it mattered. He saw no reason to explain that in a sense he was masquerading, wearing a uniform not his own. That was no one's business, and such a disclosure would undoubtedly lead to trouble.

The barber required only a little encouragement to regale him with much of the local history which had taken place since his going away half a decade before.

"Mostly, things have been kind of quiet here, leastways in comparison with what I reckon you've been accustomed to," he observed, and there was something oblique and sly in his tone and his glance. "But things do happen. I reckon you knew about your Ma's passin' a couple of years after you left. She hadn't been well for quite a while. Sort of pined – maybe worryin' about you. She was a mighty fine woman – mighty fine."

19

"Your Pa soon followed her. By then, manpower was getting mighty scarce, which caused problems, but your brother Tom managed to keep the place up, even with that bad arm of his." The arm had been broken when he had fallen from a horse as a boy, and had been stiff and partially useless since. "Quite a job for him, but he managed – till that accident about a year ago."

"Accident?" Montana repeated.

"Didn't you know? Team ran away; wagon tipped over. When they found him, he was pinned under the box, pretty bad stove up. He's just gettin' so he can walk now. Threw his crutches away no more'n a week back."

"I've had no news for a couple of years," Montana explained tightly. "Is he here in town?"

"Yeah. Had to have a lot of nursin'. Reckon he'll be glad to see you."

That would explain in part what Montana had seen the day before. With Tom helpless, the ranch would be taken over. Accidents happened – or sometimes they were contrived.

"So, with him helpless, Watson moved in."

Porter nodded wheezily, his gaze drifting from the tight set of Abbott's jaw to the handsome uniform with awe and respect.

"Yeah, Watson sort of took over," he acknowledged. "He gave out that he'd

20

bought the outfit, for debts, through old Judge MacKinnon. Tom, he claims it was cheatin', and not legal. But I guess he was so sick he was out of his head for a while."

"MacKinnon, eh," Montana repeated. "I'll have to have a word with him. He still have the same office?"

The tone, like the question, was quiet, but Porter's jowls quivered at the sharp backward jerk of his head. He remembered reacting in much the same fashion, many years before, to the sudden warning of a rattlesnake coiled almost at his feet.

"Yeah – the judge hangs out at the same place." Porter's voice took on a note of relief. "There's Tom now, comin' down the street."

3

Montana moved quickly to the door, then paused. Familiar as he was with the ravages of illness, this was shocking. Tom Abbott looked and moved like an old man, hobbling in the sun. He halted with slow disbelief as Montana stood before him, raising a hand as though to clear his eyes. His voice was barely more than a whisper.

"Bill!" he said. "It ain't – it can't be!"

It was easy to understand how Watson had taken over the ranch, but hope began to renew itself in Tom's eyes once he was assured that he was not the last of the Abbotts, and a dead end, at that. They crossed the weed-grown street to Charley's Place, watched covertly by furtive eyes. The restaurant looked run down, matching everything else in Texas. A long strand of cobweb dangled from the ceiling, picked out by the sun's rays as they were filtered by a dirty window. The lower pane had been broken and replaced with a cracked board. The screen door was rusty and full of holes, so that flies clustered about the table.

There were two customers besides themselves, one a lean and hungry-looking man who wolfed his food, glancing up to eye them sharply, then going back to the business in hand. The other was Judge MacKinnon, grayer, portly, resembling a not too sleek badger. With a napkin tucked under his triple chins, he was clearly enjoying the repast set before him. He was alone at a small table, on which was food enough to serve several. It was apparent that MacKinnon, contrary to the rule, had prospered.

He directed a brief glance their way, nodding slightly to Tom, eying Montana with no sign of recognition. It was not

22

until old Charley emerged from the kitchen, stumping on a wooden peg, and exclaimed, that the judge looked up again, then choked on a mouthful of steak.

"You gentlemen want dinner?" Charley began. Then his voice changed to a mixture of surprise, disbelief and welcome. "Bill Abbott – I beg pardon, suh! Cap'n Abbott!"

"How are you, Charley?" Montana stood and extended his hand, warming to the cordiality of the old man's beaming face. "Sure, bring us something good, Charley."

"I'll do that, Major, and it's a pleasure to welcome you back. We – what I mean is, some folks were beginning to wonder, it being so long, and not having heard from you –"

"It's a long way from Virginia to Texas," Montana returned, "especially by way of Montana." He was aware of the sudden taut silence as he added the last, and Charley glanced expectantly toward the judge, then stumped back to the kitchen.

MacKinnon scraped his chair back, whether to call a greeting or make a sudden departure was unclear. Thinking better of it, he went on with his meal, a man clearly ill at ease. Presently he sidled out, leaving a slab of pie untouched, his plate only half-emptied.

"Looks like the judge wasn't too hungry

today," Tom observed, and his voice was stronger, more confident. "He usually enjoys his food and eats for another half-hour."

"What happened to you – and the ranch, Tom?" Montana asked.

It was the sort of story he expected, which was already becoming all too commonplace not only in Texas but through much of the southland. While he lay too ill to resist, Watson had moved in and taken over. MacKinnon had provided an aura of legality with sonorous phrases and the claim of a mortgage, long overdue.

"But Pa never put any such mortgage on the land," Tom said angrily. "I know that. But I couldn't do anything, and now –" He shrugged; then his tone changed. "Now that you're back, maybe something can be done."

"We'll get the ranch back," Montana promised. "You'll be able to run it again."

"Why not the two of us? I was hoping you'd stay –"

His voice trailed off on an uncertain note. Montana shook his head.

"It's your ranch," he said. "I'll be heading back North one of these days."

"Meaning that it wouldn't support more than one of us? I guess you're right. Men are cattle-poor, with no market. Now they're being killed for their hides, and at that, they're hardly worth the trouble."

"They tell me there's a market in Missouri, Tom. Low prices for beef, but good enough to make you well off if you took a herd and sold it there."

Tom smiled tiredly.

"I'm in no shape to make such a drive," he pointed out. "Even if I was, there's a catch to that. Quite a few ranchers have tried to reach that market. Mighty few have succeeded."

Montana knew what he meant. Missouri was a long way off, and such a drive to market would have to be made through a wild and inhospitable land; country infested with men as wild as the mavericks, outlaws, scourings from both armies, who exacted a price from any who sought to cross range which they arrogantly proclaimed as their own. At best, their toll was so heavy as to wipe out any profit. More often than not, the outlaws took entire herds, murdering the drovers.

The hungry-looking man scraped his chair around to join in the conversation.

"That's for sure," he observed bitterly. "If it was just a case of getting a herd and driving it to market, I could be rich, 'fore the summer's over. There's cattle for the taking, and men and horses for the job. But

25

there's no use even thinking about driving to that market. Everybody knows how those varmints work. Somewhere along the route, they strike. All they have to do is wait, and pick and choose. They got all the advantage, and those renegades are meaner'n a blind rattlesnake. Most men with any sense would rather stay poor than die in such fashion."

"Such as?" Montana prompted.

"Such pretty little tricks as crucifyin' a man on a wagon wheel – then setting the wheel a-rollin'! Or stakin' a man out alongside a rattler, the snake staked just beyond strikin' distance of his face, with a rawhide thong run through a cut in its skin, just back of the head. Havin' such a critter jump at you can be bad enough, but finally the thong stretches, or the skin tears – things like that."

Charley edged in from the kitchen. "But why?" he asked. "What possible excuse is there for such savagery?"

"Mister, most of those outlaws have been killers for so long that they like it. And they're so far beyond the pale of the law that they can't ever go back to a decent life." His eyes flicked palely over Montana with a strange gleam; then he went on, "So that gives them a chance to take out their pizen hate on anybody they can catch."

26

He added another, even more convincing reason.

"Generally they know that anybody coming up from Texas is as poor as Job's turkey. But just supposin' a man has a lot of luck, and gets all the way, sells his stock, and has a pile of money to take back. How is he to get it back past them vultures? A man can try hidin' it – maybe hollow out a place in the wagon frame, or even have false soles on a pair of boots. I reckon a fellow could come up with any number of ingenious methods to hide the stuff. But the ways they have of loosenin' a man's tongue –" He shivered.

"You know of anybody that such things have actually happened to?" Charley persisted.

"I've talked to a couple. Somehow they lived to get back, but not much longer. Most never make it back. Oh, it's a bad nest of devils, all across that country. There's the Border Witch – and Abbott –" he stared hard, his gaze unchanging, then went on – "and plenty others, each a little meaner'n the rest."

Abruptly he turned and left the restaurant. Montana did not inquire concerning this renegade namesake. He had not missed the suspicion, the implication that, turning up after a long absence, coming down from that same country, he might be one of the outlaws.

Already he had made up his mind. His first job was to get Tom back on the old ranch, back in business. There was just one way really to put him on his feet again. He would take a herd to Missouri. There were big risks, as the hungry man had pointed out, but with the dangers were compensations.

There would come a time when the Yankee government would take care of such predators, putting a stop to outlawry, but that day was not yet. After the disorganization of war, with large sections of the country in ruin, law and order could not be restored in a day. When that happened, the markets would be open. But then the vast herds would move fast and freely, and the market would be flooded; prices would plummet. Now was the time to cash in – for anyone able or bold enough to get cattle to an eager market.

Having survived the years of war, Montana figured he was as tough as any of the lawless breed. Where there was dying to be done, at least it would not be one-sided. He would get a herd through.

He had an added advantage – some knowledge of the general route. Not only had he come down through that lawless land this spring, but he had traveled much of that stretch as a youth, before the eruption of war. Such knowledge might make all the difference.

"We'll go talk with the judge," he informed Tom, "get you back on the ranch; then I'll round up a herd and take it to Missouri."

4

Montana stood and looked about in the sharp wash of the sunshine, Tom beside him. Some of his confidence was transferring itself to his brother. Even so, it was a strange homecoming. He was aware of the sharp, suspicious scrutiny which his fancy revolvers attracted, and it came to him that he was definitely under suspicion as this outlaw named Abbott who was a terror of the strip. It would be a waste of breath either to explain or deny the identification.

They moved to MacKinnon's office, finding it empty. Zeb Porter, moving past, paused.

"Likely you'll find him in The Texas," he suggested. "I saw him duck in there, soon as he came out from eatin'. Usually he waits till the middle of the afternoon for a drink, but mebby he's worked up a thirst."

The big saloon was all but empty.

MacKinnon was at a small table, a half-empty bottle before him. He started nervously at sight of the Abbotts, then seized the bottle for a long deep gulp. He was wiping his mustache, looking up uneasily at their approach. Shoving back his chair, he got uncertainly to his feet.

"Uh – it's Captain Abbott, isn't it? This is indeed a surprise, suh – a pleasant one, of course. Particularly for you, eh, Tom? Welcome back to Texas, Captain. Is there something I can do for you gentlemen?"

"Why, yes, there is. There are matters to be talked over, MacKinnon." Montana ignored the outthrust hand, as pointedly omitting the complimentary title of "Judge." "I hope my return didn't spoil your appetite," he added.

"Spoil my – heh, heh, now that's a good one. But this is a surprise. Somehow I couldn't believe that my eyes were not playing tricks on me. It has been generally accepted in the community, suh, that you were not coming back – though the name of Abbott has not been forgotten nor neglected." He tempered the illusion with a suave shrug. "I mean, many of our gallant lads who marched away have failed to return."

"Would that belief, or hope, on your part be the reason you turned the A Bar over to Watson?"

30

Though he clearly had been fearing some such question, the bluntness seemed to upset MacKinnon.

"Turn the ranch over to Watson? I did not exactly turn it over to him, suh. Acting as your legal representative, *in absentia,* and Tom's, also Watson's – but let us repair to my office, where we can discuss matters more privately."

"We went there and didn't find you," Montana returned. "Apparently you were hoping to dodge us. So this will serve for what I have to say to you. You were our legal representative, first for our father, then for my brother and myself; that I concede. But that gave you no right to sell or turn the ranch over to the Watsons, as you appear to have done."

"I felt that it was necessary to take some action, with Tom incapacitated. The ranch could not be left vacant and untended."

"Why not? Plenty of others have been, and are. What sort of a deal did you make with Watson?"

"There was no deal, suh." MacKinnon glanced longingly at the bottle, but resisted the temptation to take it up. "Mr. Watson being the holder of the mortgage against the property, with payment long overdue, he simply foreclosed and took possession."

"That way, eh? Judge, you've grown fat

31

and sloppy with easy living. You're by way of contradicting yourself, twisting yourself up."

"I don't know what you mean. I'm merely telling you what has happened."

"There's a new term in our vocabulary, one I first heard only the other day. You'll perhaps be familiar with it. It's carpetbagger, meaning scoundrel. But it appears that not all carpetbaggers are Yankees."

MacKinnon bristled, affronted but striving unsuccessfully to regain his dignity.

"Suh, I resent the implication —"

"Resent and be damned," Montana said bluntly. "You've grown fat and affluent while most Texans have lost their shirts. Since you long since quit representing the Abbotts or the interests of justice, I see that I'll have to do some foreclosing and taking possession on my own."

MacKinnon made a valiant try to regain his dignity.

"I will overlook the personal affront, suh, due to the uniform you wear. But I must warn you that any attempt to take the law into your own hands will only lead to trouble."

"This is exactly what I intend," Montana assured him, and looked about. Perhaps it was the heat of the afternoon, or it might be that word of his return had spread and men were gathering out of heightened interest. All at once the long low room was half-filled with men who watched and listened greedily as he taunted MacKinnon. He had no need of open commendation to be sure that they liked what he was saying, or to be sure that the tolerance with which MacKinnon had once been regarded had been replaced by active dislike.

"It took me quite a while to get back," he added, and raised his voice. "For those of you who may not know me, I'm Montana Abbott, Tom's brother. I'm going out to Tom's ranch to take possession again. Tom will require a crew to run it – good cowhands, honest men, Texas men. Right now we're all in pretty much the same fix – land and cattle-poor, with mighty little money for anyone unless they belong to a certain stripe, by contrast with which a polecat is respectable. But by fall, the A Bar will have money, and we'll pay hard cash to those we hire, once we get it. Anybody interested?"

The reaction surprised and disappointed him. There was a sudden uneasy silence, a shuffling of feet. It was one thing for a man who had been counted dead to return, to offer a challenge to a lawyer who had succumbed to the prevailing segment of a new society and prospered, while others sank ever deeper in a morass of hardship. That they

33

could applaud. But his forthright challenge to them was different. They were not eager to become involved.

For the most part, these men represented the twilight society of the war years; men unfit for battle, either on account of age, physical disability or any inclination to stay as far away from trouble as possible. They might dislike their present situation, but not enough actively to involve themselves in trouble – which was what he had asked.

The name of Abbott had long been respected along the San Saba, and the Abbott spread had been counted the finest in half of Texas. Also, the uniform of a captain of cavalry, even though the Confederacy was a lost cause, was a badge of honor.

But the other side of the coin was not to be overlooked. The Watsons were just as well known, and uneasily respected. Moreover, Jabez Watson was in possession. Every man there was sharply aware of what lost causes amounted to.

Montana had been with fighting men so long that he'd expected a different reaction, but was not going to get it. They lost interest, looking everywhere but at him. His headache, temporarily forgotten in the press of events, throbbed again. Only one man pushed forward, boots clomping noisily.

34

It took a moment to recognize Abe Frost.
He had altered with the years, and in a
physical sense not for the better. He actually
wore only one boot, the other limb ending in
a wooden peg. His hair had whitened, and
there were lines deep-etched about mouth and
cheeks. Frost had been a member of the crew
when Montana had ridden away. Apparently
he'd followed to the wars, returning minus
a leg. Despite the signs of suffering and
hardship, the old light glinted under bushy
eyebrows.

"Welcome back, Cap'n," he intoned. "I
don't reckon that I'm hardly worth my salt
these days – nor does anybody else. But what
there is of me – well, I cain't think of a better
way to die!"

5

Montana gripped Frost's outstretched hand,
finding it as hard and sinewy as ever. Here
was friendship as well as loyalty.

"We won't be riding with that in mind," he
said. "Not for our side, anyway."

Abe blinked, swiping a ragged sleeve across
his face.

35

"These blasted flies," he muttered. "The way they pester, it must be makin' up for a storm –"

By the time they left The Texas, Montana had a second recruit. He was the gaunt man who had been in Charley's Place, and he was as forthright as Frost.

"If you've a job open, I can use it," he said. Anything that carries a chance for regular meals. I'll try and earn that much." He added noncommittally, "Mostly I'm called Curley."

Montana gave him a closer appraisal. Curley wore a heavy handgun, the sort of weapon which had been dubbed by some as a hog-leg. In appearance as well as power, it amounted to a hand cannon. Curley had added an innovation of his own, new to Montana. A leather thong fastened the holster down, and Montana was quick to appreciate the advantage. In a quick draw, the holster was less apt to flip about or catch, spoiling one's aim. That in itself was a clue to Curley's profession.

His glance would come as straight as an aimed gun, but would shift uneasily. His shirt was butternut, his pants the faded blue of a Yankee uniform.

Outside, tied in a patch of shade, both had horses. These, plus the contents of their duffle bags, comprised their worldly goods.

36

"As soon as I can pick up a saddle for my mule, we'll ride," Montana informed them.

Tom eyed him wistfully. He was in no condition to go along, but was clearly itching to do so.

Montana watched his crew's reaction to the idea of the three of them challenging such a contingent as took Watson's wages. Curley's glance flicked in and away, but he only hitched up his pants. Frost nodded.

"I still aim to ride," he returned.

Montana's big mule turned its head to survey him reproachfully as he tightened the girth of an old saddle. Not for a long while had it known the indignity of a cinch or the added weight and sweat, but it was a beast resigned to tribulation. Montana gave a yank, dropped the stirrup in place, and turned to find Curley staring across the street, in his eyes manifest disapprobation.

Montana stared, and surprise hit him, along with recognition. Half a decade had wrought a change in Cynthia Cartright, much but not all for the better. He remembered Cindy as a long-legged tomboy, hair flying in the sun, bronze in its brightness, a softer rust in the shade. Her blue eyes reflected the sky, and her riding habit had usually been askew. She was three years his junior, the only girl in a family of five brothers. The

37

Double T had been both a good neighbor and a fine outfit.

It came to him that he had heard nothing of Cindy or the Double T in all those years, did not know if they had prospered or failed. Cindy was putting a foot in a stirrup, reining a prancy cayuse sharply about and swinging up lightly. Her hair was as loose as ever, with the same glint, matching the color in her cheeks, the sparkle of fine teeth. She was eye-filling, breathtaking – and then he recognized the reasons for Curley's disapproval.

Curley might be an outlaw; probably he was. He was certainly as hard-bitten as they came. But where women were concerned he clung to the customs and traditions of a day which was suddenly as dead as the cause for which the South had fought. Any departure from such customs, particularly on the part of a woman, shocked him.

It startled Montana also, for this was the first time he had seen a woman in Levis, and in addition, she wore a studded cartridge belt about her slender waist. She also had a six-shooter at her hip. Gone was the modish riding habit, and with it, of course, the prosperity of the old days. Cindy had adapted to the world, not as it had been, but as it was.

It bespoke the tempo of the times, even

38

here in the heart of Texas, that she found it necessary to go armed.

She made a striking picture, reining her dancing horse under control, and now she had seen him. She looked for a moment, clearly surprised, her eyes widening, not quite believing what she saw. Then she swung alongside, leaning down with a smile as she extended a hand – one as brown as his own, the palm hard and callused.

"Bill Abbott! You're alive – you're back! Oh, Bill, it's good to see you."

"Now it seems like home, Cindy," he returned, "being welcomed by you!"

She probably had a multitude of questions, but even as a child, she had been practical. She swept a calculating glance across his companions and drew her own conclusions.

"You're heading for the A Bar," she guessed.

Montana nodded. "Seems like there's some things need attending to, what with Tom being laid up the way he has been."

Cindy studied him carefully, noting the uniform. Her eyes sparkled, then became grave.

"If you'd like any assistance –" she began tentatively.

"Why, thanks," Montana returned. "But I figure to manage."

"I don't need to remind you that Jabe Watson plays rough," she pointed out, "and a lot more so now than when you knew him. He's been the kingpin hereabouts for quite a while; also, he's hand in glove with these new locusts swarming down from the north. So, such law as there is, he controls."

It was clear that she was not afraid of Watson or the carpetbaggers, though bystanders who had tarried to watch and listen suddenly looked uncomfortable at her outspokenness and sidled away. The South had stood up to four years of strife; had it taken what passed for peace, men like Watson, to break its spirit?

"I'll remember," Montana promised, and watched her rein away. He swung onto the mule, and saw Abe Frost mount up, settling his peg leg into a specially constructed leather socket fastened to the stirrup. Abe broke the silence as they left the town behind.

"A mighty fine woman, Cindy Cartright," he observed. "Keeps the old place going, somehow. Does a man's work, and no complaining."

Curley's tone still held disapproval.

"A woman shouldn't wear the garments of men or ride astraddle," he pronounced.

Frost rounded on him.

"You're yappin' without knowing what

you're talking about," he said angrily. "Miss Cindy was raised on one of the biggest, finest ranches in all of Texas – and brung up to be a lady. Which she is. One girl, with five brothers. They all five went off to war, and not a one came back. So just what'd you have her do – fold her hands and let the place go to the devil, like most have done; or marry a hound like Watson, throwing herself in as something to boot, along with the land? Or work to save it, the way she's doing – even if it is a losing fight?"

Montana listened with interest, liking what he heard. Silence settled until he broke it.

"We may get shot at when we reach the ranch," he pointed out. "If you don't like taking such a risk, of course you're under no obligation to come along."

Frost had been worrying a brown plug with stumps of teeth. He ejected a blob of juice.

"This show is one I wouldn't miss, not for gravy or glory," he grunted. "I got a few bones to pick myself. I ain't forgetting how Watson kicked me and the other boys off."

"I take it that he just moved in, then made the A Bar his headquarters?"

"That's right. Better buildings, of course, better all around than what he'd had. He'd been eying it ever since you left. Passed the

41

remark that his place needed a lot of fixing up, so it'd be cheaper to take over."

Curley ventured a reflective opinion.

"Course, it ain't none of my business – except for me taggin' along – but it strikes me that we'll be sort of outnumbered when it comes to arguin' the question."

Frost favored him with a crooked grin.

"That's because you don't know the cap'n," he pointed out. "Reports have been drifting back for years about how he made fools of the Yankees. Long before that, he made a trip up through what they're calling The Nations these days, while he was still just a kid. Later, he went off to help Gin'ral Lee. If'n it hadn't been for starving us out, the Yanks never could have won, no matter how many extra men they had. It ain't numbers that counts."

Several men were loitering near the ranch buildings as they came in sight. It was as though Watson had anticipated the visit and was taking no chances.

Watson emerged from the adobe, then crossed to the open gate of the corral and stood to watch their approach. Legs spread wide, thumbs hooked in a heavy cartridge belt, he was a solid, paunchy figure, emanating an air of power and authority. A graceful, slightly built man came around the corner of the barn and took up a position not far away. They were like a fox and a grizzly bear.

"That's Anson – Alabama," Frost explained. "He's Watson's foreman – also his watchdog an' gunman. Between them, they're as tricky as a river-boat gambler with Yankee upbringing."

Montana pulled up, but remained in the saddle. The big mule took it upon himself to bray a hoarsely raucous greeting. Watson fell back a pace, startled and suspicious

"What the devil –" he began angrily, then recovered. "What do you jackasses want?" he challenged.

"He must have figured he recognized an old friend," Montana observed in a mild aside. "The question is, Watson, what are you doing on Abbott land?"

Watson's shrug was elaborate. "So you're back, Abbott. Everybody figured you dead – or outlawed. As for this – it's my ranch now."

"All the carpetbaggers aren't Yankees, or from the North, are they?" Montana asked. "But I'm here to tell you that this is one time when such methods won't work. This is Tom's ranch, and we're taking it back."

Laughter gusted from barrel-like lungs in a contemptuous outburst, the effect somewhat spoiled as the big mule again let loose with a bray of his own.

43

"Now is that so?" Watson's face was like old beefsteak. Clearly he believed that Montana had some way of inducing such disrespect from his mule. "I'm treatin' you with the respect due a man who's fought for the South, also remembering that this *was* your place. But things have changed." He advanced a deliberate pace.

"This land, and the stock on it, were mortgaged by your Pa, plumb to the hilt. That mortgage came due a couple of years, but I gave your brother extra time. It didn't do no good. He only got in deeper, and when he got hurt, and wasn't able to run things, I didn't have no choice but to take over. Even at that, with cattle a glut on the land and the land next to worthless, I'm left holding the sack."

Montana dismounted, and his companions followed suit. Watson's crew were scattered about, at least seven besides Alabama Anson and their boss. Montana was not surprised to observe that they were not only hardbitten but looked physically able. Beyond much doubt, they were like their employer, men who had not risked life or limb on the battlefield, even though they had few scruples as regarded fighting or killing. It was like finding himself in a nest of rattlesnakes.

"Now I know you're lying, Watson," he

44

returned. "I had a letter from my Dad a couple of years ago – one of the last I ever received. He wrote it just before he died, and in it he assured me that the ranch and herds were clear of debt, not a dollar of any sort or any mortgage against a thing. And he said that he was going to keep it that way! Moreover, he was no liar!"

Watson's face matched a gobbling turkey's, then lost color as Montana elaborated. He tried to bluster.

"When it comes to lying, I reckon you're an expert on the subject," he sneered. "As to just who's done the lying, I ain't saying, but it ain't me –"

Alabama's fox-like regard had been on Montana, speculative, puzzled and faintly uneasy. Now his face changed. He muttered something to his employer under his breath. Montana caught what sounded like his own name, and with it, the word "Border."

The effect on Watson was surprising. He flicked a startled glance at his henchman, swung it back to Montana, and his face altered from a mottled red to a dusty gray as he looked at the fancy guns riding Montana's hips. He gulped.

"Abbott," he muttered, and the tone was incredulous. "Pearl-handled guns – gold –"

His legs propelled him backward, as if of

their own volition. Again he swallowed.

"I – er – maybe we ought to discuss this a little more – talk matters over and get things straight," he suggested. "Let's step around behind the barn where we can talk, Abbott."

Whatever Alabama had implied, Watson was clearly as impressed as he was surprised. Montana nodded. He caught the warning head shake of Frost, but followed as Watson led the way. There was danger here, and treachery, but he'd come with the certainty that there would be. Probably the uniform had obtained him a hearing, a few moments of grace. Beyond that, he was on his own. Now the odds would lengthen like the afternoon shadows.

Watson halted in the shade, wheezing as if from a hard run.

"Reckon this is as good a place as any," he observed, and as his tone changed, Montana saw the plan. Alabama was sidling around the opposite end of the barn, and both he and Watson were going for their guns, driven by desperation. Watson's words were the signal.

They had him whipsawed, and their methods were as direct as they were crude. The only difference between them and a pair of diamondbacks was that, unlike the rattlers, they struck without warning.

46

6

The fancy guns at his hips were untested as
far as Montana was concerned. He'd had
no chance to do more than look at them,
feeling their balance as he slipped them from
the holsters, looking to make sure that the
chambers were loaded. How accurately they
would shoot was still to be discovered.

Now he had to find out in a hurry. Any
imperfections, such as faulted an occasional
weapon, might prove fatal. But the range
was short and direct, and he knew how to
handle six-guns. During the war years they
had become his favorite weapon.

Watson was confident of his own
skill, coupled with Alabama's speed and
ruthlessness. The odds were to their liking,
and they were losing no time in forcing a
show-down. Montana, alive, had become a
threat; if he were dead, they would again
be masters of the situation, of that whole
section of country. There could be no middle
ground.

A cow bawled in the distance. Closer at
hand, the murmur of water sounded where
the creek slipped by, just out of sight. They

were pleasant noises, long associated with his boyhood home.

The man who had traded clothes with him, whose guns these had been, had apparently put his trust in numbers; that was not Montana's way. It might come in handy to have an extra weapon in reserve, but one was all that he could use to good advantage at one time. How well, his opponents were to learn.

Alabama Anson was the faster, as his fox-like grace and manner suggested, though Watson had speed coupled with deadliness. Anson's gun barrel came clear of the leather as Montana fired. Not waiting to observe the effect of his shot, Montana swung and triggered again, and the roar of two guns, Watson's and his own, seemed to crash and mingle. Lead smashed into one of the logs of the barn, heart-high, ripping glancingly, flinging splinters in a futile shower.

Montana paused, gun at the ready, his glance swinging from one to the other. A jet of smoke, soft as the curl of mist above a creek at dawn, spilled from the gun's muzzle.

Alabama was writhing on the hard-packed earth, pain and fright and a certain recognition and resignation struggling across his face. His gun had fallen and lay forgotten, as he pressed a hand to the flow of blood from his upper right leg. The red was staining the gun belt and the shirt, spattering over the heavy cowhide chaps.

Watson was retreating, staggering backward as though his legs had lost all volition of their own. He brought up against the side of the barn and leaned there, his face twisted haggardly. Blood dripped along his elbow, forming an uneven rivulet down the sleeve before dribbling off the splayed-out fingers. His revolver had fallen into a pocket of dust, where a horse or bull had pawed not many days before. Stirred, the film sifted over the bright sheen of the barrel, obscuring the curl of smoke.

There came a rush of feet, boots pounding on the hard ground, men swarming around both corners of the barn, some with fingers crooked for a fast draw. They checked with an almost comical abruptness, staring, for now both guns were in Montana's hands, menacing them in an ungentle warning. With his back to the barn, he controlled the situation. Frost and Curley prowled at the rim of the circle, ready and watchful.

"There has been enough shooting," Montana pronounced harshly. "We've had a settlement. But there's nothing like keeping the peace," he went on, and his mustaches lifted. "So, just to be sure, you'd better get their guns, Abe. We'll put your hardware in a

49

sack and dump it at The Corners, and you can pick it up later."

He waited while Frost followed instructions. Two or three of Watson's crew were hesitant, of half a mind to resist, but they had made the mistake of all coming at once, rushing full into the sweep of leveled guns. There was no one left who might sneak up from cover.

"I could have killed you, Watson," Montana informed him. "And I didn't refrain because you haven't got it coming. But I've had over much of killing. So saddle and ride, all of you. And don't come back. Tom will be here again, with a crew. Should it be necessary, so will I!"

Watson kept his eyes on him as though fascinated. He was at a loss to understand clemency, knowing that he would have given none. But for the moment, at least, he was not inclined to argue.

At Montana's suggestion, their wounds were bandaged, and Alabama was able to stand, then to mount painfully onto a horse. His hurt was more painful than serious. Watson's arm had fared less well. The bone was broken. Once it healed, it would probably be so stiff that he'd have no more use of it for a fast or treacherous draw.

Presently they were gone, riding out like the

fading of a bad dream. Frost and Curley eyed Montana with an increased respect verging on awe.

"Abbott of the Border," Frost muttered under his breath. "I reckon that explains a lot of things. What now, Cap'n?" he added, raising his voice.

"Let's see if we can rustle up some grub," Montana suggested. "As the wolf growled to the bobcat, 'Meals are spotty.' "

Frost busied himself in the kitchen, and Montana prowled the house as he cooked, holding his emotions under a tight rein. There was much that was old and familiar, but too much dirt and disorder from the occupancy of the invaders. It was as though, not really expecting to remain permanently, they had fouled the nest.

On the whole, he was satisfied. Both his return to Texas and today's expedition had been gambles, and he'd won them, as much from surprise as anything else. But taking the ranch back was only a beginning. Tom was well on the road to recovery, and his morale was pretty well restored. He'd probably be able to hold the land. But one more island of poverty in the midst of a defeated and impoverished country would be of little real help, either to Tom or his neighbors.

The only way really to put the ranch on

a paying basis, to give Tom a chance, was to take a herd to market. That most men considered that impossible was a challenge. If it was accomplished, it would change the outlook for most of Texas.

Getting back the ranch was only half the job. It must be finished before he could feel right about heading back to Montana.

Frost cooked a surprisingly good meal, stumping about briskly, helping himself to supplies such as had long been out of the reach of most Texans. There were biscuits, made of white flour, the first that Curley admitted to tasting in years. Montana mopped up the gravy with a biscuit, realizing that his accusations had been accurate. Only someone who sided with the carpetbaggers who now ruled the country could have obtained such luxuries.

Their hunger satisfied, it was time to get back to town. Trouble had a way of catching up, once a man slowed down.

"All right, but what about this?" Frost made a wide gesture, which took in not only the house but also the ranch. "You aiming to let them come back?"

"Not if we can help it. Once we report that we have the ranch, you shouldn't have much trouble picking up a crew. I figure there are a lot of honest men who'll jump at the chance,

52

once they see there is a chance. Pick men you like and can trust; then get back here and move in. Tom will be with you – and until he is strong again, I expect you to hold the fort."

A pleasurable excitement brightened the leathery planes of Abe's face. Such trust, coupled with responsibility, were more than he had expected.

"You figure I can handle such a job?"

"I figure you can." Montana made the statement without elaboration. "You'll be busy, and there'll be a living in it – and that's about all, till I can get a herd to Missouri and get the money back to you. After that, things should be better."

Plenty of men would be willing to work for their keep, since nothing better was available – with the hope of fair wages once the drive proved a success. But that seemed more a dream than a promise, bright as a rainbow but just as nebulous.

"You really aiming to try and take a herd up there?" Frost asked disbelievingly. "It's a mighty chancy trip – and getting back with the money could be even worse."

"Somebody has to," Montana reminded him. "We can't simply go on starving or being bluffed."

"Well, I reckon that's right," Frost admitted. "But you'll be gambling not only your herd but your life."

Montana did not remind him that life had been counted as among the cheapest of commodities during the years just past. Though the price often came high, things precious and worth-while could sometimes be purchased. But he knew what Frost meant. A number of men, driven as much by desperation as by the hope of reward, had made just such a try as he proposed. They had been fighting men, trained in a hard school.

For some months now the tally, or lack of it, had been coming in. Reports filtered back of death and disaster; or else, even more grim, there was no news at all. And no money. Bleaching bones across a wasteland marked the end of once high hopes.

The odds, even with a good crew, would be heavily stacked against them. Montana was under no illusions.

Curley studied him obliquely as they rode. There was something far back in his eyes, deep as a whirlpool – a mixture of doubt tinged with hope. He made up his mind.

"If you take that trip, I'd like to go along."

"Why, now, I was hoping you'd feel that way about it," Montana agreed.

He needed the encouragement of Curley's offer and the faith it implied in the days which followed. The news of how he had dealt with Watson, retaking the A Bar, sent surprise and a shock wave rippling across the range. None who had watched the trio ride out had expected such a result; most had doubted that any of them would ever come back. Men began to eye Montana with wonder and respect, even a quickening hope.

But what he proposed seemed folly on a far greater scale. It was a worthy ambition, and if he managed to achieve it, would rate as an outstanding accomplishment. The profits of such a venture would be almost fabulous. But the rub was that others would probably spend the money.

Tom was in agreement, although somewhat dubious. What grated most was that he was in no shape to make the trip.

"What you really want is to get the job done, then head back to Montana," he said shrewdly. "That country's really in your blood, isn't it?"

"It is," Montana admitted. "I'll always have a warm spot in my heart for Texas – but the real frontier's up there. It's my country."

He outlined his proposition to a representative group of citizenry – a pathetically altered group from what it would have been half a decade before. Looking over the men who did him the

55

honor of listening carefully, Montana found many once familiar faces absent, the casualties of war. Others bore the scars of conflict.

They listened, but it was hard to spark excitement or any real interest in their eyes. There was rather despair, the hopelessness which defeat and then frustration had fastened upon them. In their faces was a conviction of defeat which even the surrender of Lee had not been able to place there.

But Montana would not admit to being licked before he started. There had to be a way to get others to ride with him.

"Tom is putting in a thousand head of his cattle," Montana told them. "We could make up the entire herd, as far as that goes, but I want this to be a neighborhood venture, with quite a few outfits involved. I'll need extra men, extra backing, and I want as many of you as possible to share in the profits, so that this whole section of range can recover.

"Also, we'll need three wagons – good solid ones – for the chuck wagon and to tote the necessary supplies. Tom is furnishing one from the ranch – the only good wagon on it. But one is not enough. Others can contribute cattle and men for the crew, and the extra wagons. We'll take care of the supplies."

He would be doing that. That final contribution was not only customary, but necessary. Montana was certain that none of the others could scrape together anything other than cattle, men or a possible wagon. They had no money, no credit with which to buy, nor would such a nebulous prospect as lay ahead win them any. But thanks to a dead man, he had enough gold for the bare necessities.

He proposed to start the drive as soon as the necessary men and supplies could be readied. Cattle would pose no problem.

They had found a new wagon on the A Bar, further proof that Watson was in with the carpetbaggers. Otherwise, it seemed doubtful that a new wagon had been sold or purchased anywhere along the San Saba since the first guns had sounded at Fort Sumpter. Texas men had marched to join the cause, but Texas itself had become a backwater, stagnant and isolated, falling into disrepair.

Old vehicles, on two wheels or four, still held together, by dint of much repairing and wiring, along with soaking of wheels. But such wagons would not do for the trail. On such an expedition, endurance was vital.

Still, a couple of others should be available, and a joint enterprise was essential to success. But the outlook was bleak. One man was more frank than most.

"I'd like to go in with you on such a

proposition, Captain – like to go along. Only I ain't got the nerve to risk it. Reckon I'd rather starve here than die on the trail."

Montana eyed them grimly. "You can suit yourselves," he admitted. "I'm going, if I have to do it alone."

Whether that shamed them or not, there was discussion, arguments which grew animated. Some reconsidered, Sam Henson leading the way. His spread was down-river from the Bar, but it had been a big one, and still was, as far as land and cattle went.

"I'll furnish a wagon and go along," he said. "And I'll put in a thousand head."

His beard, peppered with gray, was patriarchal. Otherwise he was a vigorous man, and would be a real addition to the crew.

Captain Mulroney's considering glance ranged from Henson to Montana; then he moved from the crowd. He was a newcomer to Texas, having drifted in after the end of hostilities, acquiring an otherwise deserted spread and a brand.

"Sure and I like the sound of what ye have in mind, Abbott." He smiled. "And as you say, a man might as well be buried as dead and not knowin' it. Count on me for five hundred head, and such work as I can do along the trail."

Hackshaw, from what was counted the

back country, added another five hundred. With that, they seemed to have reached a sticking point. The three thousand head was not much of a problem in itself. It made a somewhat large bunch for the trail, but on such a venture, numbers might mean the difference between success and disaster. What he had to have were more men, so involved that they would fight for survival; and almost as important, one more good wagon.

Such a vehicle was as hard to come by as were additional volunteers. Many men from various crews already committed refused flatly to go. It was not that they were lacking in courage. Rather, as one put it, they had better sense.

Montana did not try to persuade the hesitant. The best hope of success lay in setting out with a convinced, dependable crew, men who would fight no matter what. The timid or hesitant would be no asset.

Abe Frost offered to go along, pointing out that he could still ride or use a gun, but he could not be spared from the ranch. Tom needed a dependable foreman. Several conferences left him still short of the bare minimum which he had set. No one else seemed willing to venture forth, and the fears which were more or less openly expressed had a way of communicating themselves, to cause a falling off among those already pledged.

Discouraged, Montana stepped from a conference in The Texas to the street, brilliant with the hues of sunset. It alone seemed to carry promise. Then he saw a rider coming into town at a full gallop. The horse stopped with sliding hoofs, raising a cloud of dust. Out of it emerged Cynthia Cartright, jumping down, hurrying across to him. Her voice throbbed with excitement.

"Bill Abbott, why didn't you tell me what you planned?" she demanded. "Don't I count, or aren't my cattle as good as any? I just heard about your drive today, and I think it's wonderful – the greatest thing that's happened in this part of Texas since hope died!

"You can count me in," she added. "I'll furnish a thousand head of cattle and a couple of men. And I have a new wagon, that I'd ordered months ago. It should be here in time for the drive. You can take it, too."

7

Montana was startled as well as pleased. Somehow it hadn't occurred to him to consider the Double T as a possibility, even though it was a big outfit, and Cindy had welcomed him warmly on his return. But she was a woman, and this would be a long trail and a grim one.

Yet if she wanted to risk the cattle, their loss would not be too serious should the drive fail. The wagon would be of vital importance. Her offer was a lifesaver.

"I'll sure do my best to get the herd through," he agreed, "and to get back with your share of the profits."

"I know you will." She was quietly assured. "I wouldn't risk it unless you were in charge, Bill. You've had a lot of experience, with men as well as with cattle. Also, you know something of the country in general, which is more than most of the others can say."

She eyed him approvingly. He was wearing Levis and chaps, the uniform and its implications put away. Only the fancy guns still rode at his hips.

"You look like a Texan again," she added.

"Somehow I like you better this way."

Coming from her, the compliment pleased him. Now, with the details set, the next days were busy ones, spent rounding up and gathering the various bunches of cattle into a single herd. They could be more tractable once they were lined out on the drive, long miles under their hoofs each day. Having grown accustomed to the meekly domesticated cows of Eastern and Southern farms, Montana was a bit startled at the wildness of this new breed of longhorns.

For they were a new breed, something the world had never before seen. Certain traits had become more pronounced even in the years that he had been away. Forced largely to fend for themselves, these animals had reverted to the wild. The wickedness in their massive horns matched their bad temper. As lean as wolves, they could run or fight with any creatures of the plains.

Handling them required cool nerve as well as knowledge. But at least they were ideally suited to the rigors of a long, hard drive.

Supplies were loaded in the two wagons. Everything was now in readiness except for the third wagon, which Cindy had promised, but which had not been delivered. The hardware dealer declared it should come any day.

It was needed, but Montana dared not wait. Some of the crew might get cold feet.

"Why don't you go ahead?" Cindy suggested. "As soon as it comes, I'll have it loaded and send a man with it. It will catch up with you before you get very far."

Montana agreed. A team and wagon could travel twice as fast as the herd. Looking over his assembled crew, he was reasonably satisfied. Most of them were veterans, men who had smelled powdersmoke, who were accustomed to hardship. And they were as dismayed as he was at the sort of peace to which they had returned.

Captain Mulroney arrived with his five hundred head, his quick, easy smile and ready jests, but he was not as warmly welcomed as the others had been. Some questioned why Montana had admitted him to the company.

"It could be that I'm prejudiced, and maybe without reason," Hackshaw admitted. "But he's almost too handsome for a man, and he laughs too easily, and fights too readily. And who he is or was, or where he came from, nobody knows. Some figure him to be a renegade Yankee. The boys don't trust him – and no more do I."

Montana could only shrug the protest aside, amused at the quirks of men's minds. He was suspected of being a renegade also, but

63

of supporting their side. If they knew that he'd been a Yank by adoption, wearing the despised blue uniform even against the Indians –

It was too late to alter plans or personnel, whatever the reason. And if Mulroney had stopped short of open outlawry, choosing rather to lose himself in a land as wide as Texas, that was no particular indictment. There were many others like him.

Yet he was brash and overly bold; his methods of acquiring land and stock had not been too well liked. Also, the crew he'd gathered, some of whom were riding this trail, were as wild as himself.

"Sure he's a fighting man, and that's what we need," Hackshaw added. "But what worries the boys is that, as likely as not, he's one of that gang that straddles the Border. He could side with them when it comes to a showdown."

"So could any of us," Montana pointed out. "I'll take my chances with him."

With a string of horses for his own use, Montana relegated the big mule to the A Bar and a well-earned rest. Cutting horses were vital with such a herd, animals tough, well trained, jackrabbit quick.

It could be a long drive, with the turbulent Colorado to be crossed almost before they were well started. After that would come a variety of country, much of it wild, a considerable part having reverted to wilderness during the war years. Wide stretches would be barren of water, vaguely if not actively hostile.

"We Texicans should have settled a country by ourselves," Sam Henson grumbled. "Texas is plenty big, and we'd have been a sight better off. Join the Union, then fight to get out of it – that's the same thing as drawin' a razor across your own throat. But men ain't got half the sense of geese!"

Tom, able again to sit a horse, was one of several gathered to see them off. Cindy Cartright waved from beside him, and emotion hoarsened Montana's voice as he gave the word. It was sunrise as they lined out, the cattle stepping briskly, as though conscious that adventure awaited them. His instructions were simple.

"We'll keep them moving, but allow them to pick their own pace. And keep in mind that the easiest way to drive a bunch is to let them think they're doing it all themselves. Guide; don't crowd."

It would take a couple of days to run off the eagerness, to shake them down to a steady pace, but the going should be routine until they were well above the Colorado – barring

65

trouble at the river. You could never be sure of a stream or of a herd. Or of a woman, Henson added lugubriously. All three were unpredictable.

Sixteen thousand hooves, four thousand pairs of rapier-tipped horns, represented potential wealth or certain ruin. For good or ill, they were embarked on the adventure, and there could be no turning back.

8

The river rolled, roiled and sluggish, its turbulence increased by rains somewhere along its vast watershed. The river of the ages, the Colorado contained a power which had eroded canyons of unbelievable magnitude; it could still pounce as suddenly and savagely as a puma.

On this afternoon of lowering clouds and long slanting sun, it had an ugly look, swirling, sucking with sudden undercurrents, breaking loose in spurts. To gaze upon it for a long time would give a man the jitters.

Montana allowed no time for doubt or questioning. He led the way, kicking off boots and chaps, moving fast as the van of

66

the herd neared the water and made ready to pause, to eye the broad sweep distrustfully. A shower had spilled from the still uncertain clouds, freshening the grass, taking care of thirst as the cattle grazed, so that the river held no attraction. Given time to look, they would veer away, preferring not to wet their hooves, shunning the prospect of a swim.

Montana drove in suddenly, cutting half a hundred head before they could cluster or pile up. Curley and Mulroney, shoving them to a run, brought them to the water's edge. Montana's horse took it at a gallop, the water splashing silver, and this was something to follow. The steers, unable to dodge, came right behind, swimming before they realized it. Then the main body of the herd were being fed in after them, and minutes later, Montana's horse scrambled onto the far bank.

He headed upstream and recrossed, twice more taking the lead with small bunches as gaps spread and hesitation threatened. It was tiring work, with a considerable element of risk, a sea of horns swirling at his heels all the way across. But the big herd endured its baptism and crossed over without serious incident.

The remuda was sizable, with ten horses for each man. The number of mounts was unusual, but Montana figured that the extra animals might save lives when the going grew rough.

The Colorado was hardly more than a fading memory when they faced the first real test. All at once the weather was hot and dry, and they stirred the dust across a parched range. The rains, which had been ample along the San Saba, apparently had skipped this region. Montana was faced with a problem he had not expected to encounter so early in the season: drought.

Much of this land had remained unsettled, and most of what men had tamed had reverted to wilderness. There was grass to spare, but how long there might be water for the big herd became a more worrisome question with each day's advance. How far this land of little rain might stretch there was no way of telling. Montana rode ahead, finding no answer. They would be all right as far as the chain of lakes, but after the last lake was passed, the immensity of Texas would be all about them.

"And whether we should keep straight north, or swing east or west, is pretty much a matter of guesswork," Montana admitted to the others. "A good rain, of course, would solve everything. But until something busts loose, we run the risk of going thirsty."

He fell silent, deep in introspection, recalling that earlier drive before he'd left home, the pitiless nature of a dry prairie. Almost in a whisper he went on:

"You ever try to handle cattle when they're on their last legs, choking with thirst? It's not a job I'm partial to."

But this drive had been his idea; he'd talked the others into it. There could be no turning back.

Sam Henson was equally worried, scanning a sky from which even the light clouds of summer had vanished. "Look at the grass!" he muttered. "It's nigh as powdery, when you step on it, as the ground. But I'm most worried about the grub, with that other wagon not catchin' up. Sure, a man can keep from starvin' on a meat diet, but after about so long, it can be pretty bad. And if that wagon Cindy promised don't show pretty soon, it never will."

Montana was nagged by the same thought. Something must have gone wrong. But they could not wait.

"At least there's plenty of water at the lakes," he pointed out. "Every animal can drink its fill and be in top shape for the dry stretch beyond."

There were some seven lakes, forming a

69

chain, each about a mile apart. This year they were an oasis in the middle of the desert. Beyond the final one was a stretch of some sixty miles which was usually parched, save during the rainy season. What worried Montana was how far those miles might stretch in a drought year. Flesh, whether horse or human or cattle, could endure only to a certain point.

Again he scouted ahead. The lakes were natural water holes, with rocky bottoms. Filling his canteens, riding one horse and leading another, he headed on north, moving after sundown. It was cooler, so that more miles could be covered with less strain.

There was plenty of grass, which lost its crispness and became moist with night dew. The dust-dry smell faded from his nostrils. At midnight he allowed the horses to graze for a couple of hours, benefiting from the scant moisture. The land lay wide and empty under the moon.

With daylight he estimated that he should be about at the rim of the dry stretch, and dry it had proven. Then, once the sun flamed across the prairie, he spied a patch of green far ahead and drew a breath of relief. This was as he remembered it from that journey before the war. His recollection was accurate, not a dream confused with the events of other years, hope and desire. That green meant water. It would mean hard going to reach there, but they should be able to make it.

The herd was at the final lake when he rejoined the drive. The cattle were rested, well fed, ready to go. There was still no sign of the third wagon.

They set out an hour short of sundown, pushing the herd for the first time, rather than allowing them to drift at their own pace. By morning, Montana estimated that they had crossed a third of the dry stretch. They halted, allowing the tired animals to graze, to make the most of the dew before the onrush of sun sucked it away. At mid-forenoon he put them into motion again.

Kegs had been filled at the lake, loaded into the wagons. Even with canteens, it was becoming a dry drive for men as well as animals. There was no coffee, no hot meals. The accumulated grime remained on unwashed skin. The sun, hot as a torch since they'd left the river, was suddenly oppressive, a red bowl of fury burning across the sky.

They rested through the hottest hours of the afternoon, then roused the cattle and shoved them ahead. They moved mechanically now, a domesticated herd, the spring gone from their walk, the sparkle of adventure faded

71

from dull eyes. They lowed thirstily, but there was no water, and there would be none until the sixty miles were behind them. The riders made full use of the remuda, changing mounts at frequent intervals.

All at once the pattern was reversed. Where they had crowded the herd to increase their speed, now it was necessary for the outriders to hold them back. Impatient, wild with thirst, the steers were anxious to break from a walk, to run if allowed. Montana understood and sympathized, but such a course could not be permitted. A run would quickly take on some aspects of a stampede, but only to a degree. Soon, with bodies sapped of all reserves of moisture and vitality, they would slow to a stumbling walk, then begin to fall. Once they were down, many would never regain their feet.

If held to a steady pace, they could go for a long while. The wagons circled ahead, making camp well in advance of the herd. With the sinking of the sun, the tired animals commenced to graze. Montana estimated that two thirds of the dry stretch had been covered when finally they bedded down for a brief, uneasy rest. They allowed the cattle much more room than usual, but many refused to rest, jumping up, frantic with thirst.

"It's going to be nip and tuck," Henson

observed, out of the depths of experience. "But we're not in any serious trouble – so far."

Sleep came in fitful snatches. Most of the crew had to keep riding to prevent the restless herd from straying in all directions. There was one boon. A hot meal was prepared, with coffee to wash down the food. Bone-weary men could not have kept on otherwise.

An hour before dawn, Montana again gave the word, and they moved. He appreciated the meager comfort of this coolest hour of the twenty-four, the heavier curtain of darkness. Then the rising splash of sun dissipated what scant hope they had entertained that the day might break cooler, possibly even with a curtain of clouds. If anything, it loomed out of the East as more of a scorcher than the preceding ones.

"Water casks are empty," Curley reported laconically.

Montana's lips were cracked and sore, a common affliction. The cattle moved like sleepwalkers, their lowing a mournful dirge, tongues lolling. The horses were in scarcely better shape.

"Go on to that green stretch," Montana instructed the drivers of the wagons. "With luck, we'll reach there by mid-afternoon."

There would be no midday meal, but each man had a can of tomatoes, which could be drunk as well as eaten. This final push was going to be hell on the hoof in a literal sense, but they had to keep moving.

Montana stuck with the herd, sending Curley to scout ahead and report. At a little past the sun's zenith, he was back, and the grimness of his face was not belied by either his appearance or his words. He was like a scarecrow on a skeleton horse.

"Grady met me – asked me to scout both ways," he said briefly. Grady was the cook. "The creek where that trace of green shows, has gone dry. Only mud is left. He couldn't dig to water. I traveled both ways, miles upstream, then down. Found water just once – what had been a big, deep hole."

He shook his head wonderingly.

"There'd been a lot of fish trapped there – and minks and birds after them. There were tracks everywhere in the mud, regular trails – all dry and hard now. The scavengers hadn't been able to clean them all out. There were still dead fish, even a dead mink. Even my horse wouldn't touch the dregs."

Montana heard him, appalled at the immensity of the disaster. The words were like a knell.

"Gray and his helper are still digging,"
74

Curley added, "hopin' to get water enough for the horses. I dunno."

"Sure, and there's more trouble along the trail than even I counted on," Mulroney commented, his cheerfulness diluted for once. "And I expected nothing else."

The hope was a thin one, but when they arrived the cook had found water. The trouble was that it was barely a trickle. There was no more than could be dipped half a bucket at a time to give snorting, desperately eager horses. It was a fight to control them so that they would not spill and waste what little there was. The water hole was slow in filling, so that no horse was given more than half as much as it wanted. During the night they were watered in relays. That was better than the cattle were faring.

The herd was increasingly restless, a moaning desperation driving them, so that there was no rest for the men. Montana studied the sky and prayed for clouds, for a cool day. Should that occur, they might keep going. And there had to be water before long. But the sun came blazing out of a relentless dawn, and the herd was on the verge of revolt.

By mid-morning they were feverish and unmanageable. A glimpsed oasis, apparently seen by men and animals alike, had turned out to be only a mirage. Now it was only a matter of time, and not much of that, before they stampeded or died.

9

This, above all other times, Montana realized, was when he must remain cool-headed, in order to find some solution. The trouble was that there was none. There was no water, and the herd was turning mad.

It was madness in the double sense of the word: a slowly growing anger, inspired by desperation, as well as a frenzy of sun and thirst. Men, cattle and horses had all reached the ragged edge of exhaustion. Weariness was aggravated by parched bodies and the inexorable blast of sun from a too bright sky. There was a stir of breeze, but the wind brought no relief. It stung blistered hides or skin as though coming off the nether regions. No cloud puffed even faintly across the merciless sweep of a withered world.

Until then, they had all been sustained by at least a faint hope, and that had given them a measure of control over the herd. All at once, hope and control were gone. The leaders did not arrest their movement, but they swung about, refusing to be checked or directed. For a time they had moved with apparent purpose or direction. But now they were as irresistible as a tide. When horses or hoarsely shouting men got in their way, they ignored them. The horses had to step aside or be run over. Ropes' ends across noses, even gunshots, had no effect.

Now the whole herd was milling, at first raggedly, then more and more wildly. Working together, a few men could check a wedge of the herd, but immediately afterward another mass would erupt, moving at cross-purposes. The drift was like snow tossed by twisting winds. Only here there was heat, and even the thought of a blizzard's chill breath seemed like a dream, remote and impossible.

Henson swung his horse alongside Montana's, swiping sweat from his face with a brush of his sleeve. His horse dropped its head and panted. The rancher's eyes were black with bewilderment.

"I never saw anything the like of this," he confessed. "The cattle are plumb crazy – not that I blame them. But what's got into them?"

Montana gave him a straight answer, as the truth was impressed upon him.

"They're crazy, all right," he conceded. "Also, *they're going blind!*"

Henson's eyes widened with shock. He

swung to view the cattle with fresh insight, sucking in a ragged breath.

"Blind!" he repeated. "My God! I believe you're right."

The certainty was chilling, though not of the sort to abate either heat or thirst. The long strain of thirst and exhaustion, of an overly bright sun and fever, was taking an unexpected toll. Now, obeying a common impulse, acting from instinct as well as memory, the entire herd had turned about and was taking the back trail. There had been water back at the lakes. For as long as they could stagger, they would strive to reach it again.

There was nothing to do, no possibility of controlling, stopping or even turning them. Normally docile, they were past all that, obeying the dominant urge for self-preservation. And why not? Montana thought tiredly. Everything else had failed. He had led them into a trap. Always before, there had been at least some water at this time of year. But the drought through this section was worse than anyone had thought possible. Water at the creek, where green had beckoned in a false promise, had never before been known to fail.

Such things had happened before, though not often. Not every herd that vanished on

78

the trail was rustled or stolen, nor were all bleaching bones due to treachery, to the strikes of Indians or renegades. Nature, in such a mood, could be implacable.

Montana reminded himself that he should have ridden faster and farther, checking out the country more completely before making the long hop beyond the final lake. But he'd trusted the distant evidence of greenery, the knowledge that the creek was there, and always before had been a living, viable thing.

This had probably been a fatal mistake. He looked around, trying to figure it out. He'd realized the hazards of this undertaking, the risks to be encountered, and had planned how they could be met. The one factor which he had overlooked, while still within the confines of Texas, short of all anticipated dangers, was what was happening.

"It was a dumb thing to do," he acknowledged. "For when the score is all added up, it's the weather, one way or another, that licks more men than all other troubles combined."

The wagons with their supplies were north of them now, still at the supposed oasis. Now the drifting, milling herd was finally lining out with desperate purpose.

The cook and his helper would have to use their own judgment. They could stay where they'd found a scant supply of water, or head back. Without them, men and horses faced ever mounting hazards.

The rest of them would go along with the herd. It was no longer a matter of choice. There was still a possibility that they might make it back to the last lake, at least some of the stronger ones. There was even the remote chance of a lifesaving shower somewhere along the way.

A wave of his hat brought the others. They gathered to listen, exchanging no greetings.

"Pick the strongest horses," he instructed them. "Henson, Mulroney, Curley and I will stay with the herd and keep shoving them along as well as we can. We'll do our best to keep them from falling out and dying. The rest of you are to go back to the lake and rest up when you get to water. You can help as the herd approaches the lakes."

The three he had chosen accepted this added chore without complaint, since he was staying with them. The rest of the crew jogged out of sight without looking back.

The herd had positioned itself again, straggling far worse than during the ordered drive. But they were trying, still moving. Normally only a couple of miles were allowed between the leaders and the stragglers on a regular day. Now they were strung out for three times that.

Other differences were noticeable, their implications grim. None tried deliberately to loiter, to snatch extra bites of grass or to sneak aside and rest. Those which fell out now did so from weakness, but for the most part they plodded doggedly, a mournful lowing dribbling past hanging tongues. They staggered and weaved, but they kept plodding.

Montana lost count of time. He, and the trio who remained, were akin to the cattle, their minds dulled, dazed from exhaustion, their movements a mechanical reaction. The long agony of the afternoon burned away; the sun was a red ball which seemed to hang endlessly in the sky.

Missing something, Montana roused and looked about. A horse stood, not moving, riderless. Mulroney was on the ground, legs outstretched, eyes closed. To his own surprise, Montana found a slosh of water remaining in his canteen. He dismounted, legs as clumsy as stilts, and poured the brackish liquid between Mulroney's cracked lips.

The captain's eyes opened, a puzzled light in them as he raised his head. Then he managed a cracked smile and somehow got back into the saddle.

"Sure and it's a generous man ye are, Montana," he murmured, with reference to the water. "And that the tepid stuff could be like nectar I would not have believed."

Montana swung after stragglers, hazing them back and ahead, his shouts sinking to hoarse yips which stirred the animals no more than the distant bickering of coyotes. These, as always, hung upon the fringes of the herd, faring better than usual as their victims multiplied. The cattle paid no attention to them, stirred neither by scent nor sight.

Surprisingly, they were making good time, almost the equal of an average herd under normal conditions. Montana's horse was forced to a steady gait to keep up. Desperate to reach the water which was like the rainbow's end, from somewhere they were digging up a reserve of strength.

Montana roused as darkness drifted across the range, not a heavy blackness but an obscure dimness in which the brassy sun was mercifully blotted from sight. There was some small relief, but the cattle showed no sign of stopping.

After aiding Mulroney, he had worked mechanically. Now he realized that he was alone, as far as human companionship was concerned. For a long while he had neither seen nor heard the others. Somewhere, too, he had lost his extra horse. How or when it had happened, he had no recollection.

He found some relief in walking, easing his horse. Remembering his canteens, he examined them, and was not surprised or particularly disappointed to find them empty. Emptiness was everywhere, even in the star-studded sky, which stretched endlessly, like the vastness of the prairie. Wearily he pulled himself back into the saddle.

Determinedly he tried to think, but his mind was like the cattle, plodding mechanically. Focusing his attention on the wavering rind of moon, he decided that it was past midnight. At this hour there was a pleasant coolness, in contrast to the heat of the day, even a scant dew which moistened such grass as had escaped the trampling hoofs.

Some of the cattle were responding to hunger and snatching an occasional mouthful, but none were halting to graze. The need for water overrode all else.

Despite its burden, his horse was keeping up. Everything had become part of a dream. Montana nodded in the saddle, alternately rousing, then dozing . . .

The sunshine was blinding as he opened his eyes, the first rays across the horizon slanting into his face, bringing him awake. Jolted into realization, he looked about. They should be heading south, just for the moment at least the drift of the herd was more to the east. Again, as on the preceding days, there was only an unblemished horizon, with no cloud and no promise of any in the sky.

He was past thinking clearly, though the sleep had helped. Hunger was a steady if subdued pain, and thirst had become a raging fever through every fibre of his body. He could understand and sympathize with the cattle, who had gone even longer without water.

His horse was in bad shape, still trying gamely, but staggering at intervals. His hoarse whoa was a strange sound in his own ears. He got off, nearly falling, saving himself by clutching at the saddle-horn. He managed an uncertain step or so, then, turning to lead the cayuse, stared to find that it had collapsed. The pony lay stretched on the ground, eyes rolling. They filmed as he watched.

He should show as much gumption as the horse, Montana thought tiredly, and keep going as long as he could. Most of the herd was on ahead, still finding spirit or energy to plod, though some, like the horse, were swaying, falling. Lobos quarreled now with the coyotes. He could hear them but could not make them out, and he wondered if the same blindness that afflicted the cattle was coming upon him.

Looking up was easier, but not more encouraging. Buzzards hung in the too bright sky. Others were dipping, ink blots spilling.

He took another step, his knees buckled, and he went down. He felt nothing, no longer cared. There was no apprehension concerning the winged or fanged scavengers. Nothing that belonged to the living mattered. With the dead there was rest.

10

Montana roused as if from a deep sleep. Something was drawing him back to consciousness. It was like a forgotten dream, a sense of bliss which might turn out to be a mirage, but which at the moment was powerfully impelling. He swallowed, opened his eyes, and stared in complete disbelief, reaching for the canteen held tantalizingly just out of reach.

With understanding came amazement, which overrode all else. His head was pillowed on a lap; upon a gingham apron, to be exact. And there were soft hands and a tender voice, and anxious eyes in the face bending above. He closed his eyes, shaking his head, but when he opened them again the vision persisted. He struggled to sit up, finding himself as limp as a frosted stalk.

"It's all right, Bill." The voice was Cindy's, hushed but vital. A faint smile relieved the anxiety in her face as she studied his. "You're going to be all right. Here, take another swallow – but just a swallow, now. You can have more presently."

He clutched the canteen and drank until she tugged it away. The water was life. He managed to sit up, coming out from the scant shade of Cindy and her sunbonnet, and the full, hot heat of the afternoon was like a kick in the face. But Cindy was real, and so was the big canvas-topped wagon standing nearby – canvas so new that it bore scarcely a stain – and the team which hauled the wagon.

Someone else was coming around the rear of the wagon, her face shiny with perspiration, smiling anxiously as she saw that he was conscious. Montana remembered Mandy from before the war. Born a slave, she had been given her freedom by the Cartrights years before the outbreak of hostilities. But she had loyally remained with them, regardless of the whims of fortune.

86

"Thank goodness," she breathed, and threw up both hands in a wide gesture. "I was mighty scared, there for a spell, that he wouldn't be wakin' up again, this side o' them pearly gates."

Montana felt light-headed with relief. He was not at all sure that his own retort did not show it.

"Pearly gates?" he repeated. "Seems to me like I've been at just about the opposite extreme from them, Mandy."

"Maybe yo' have, Mist' Abbott, maybe yo' have," Mandy agreed. "But lucky fo' us – an' you – we saw them buzzahd's a-circlin', an' got here in time."

Getting to his feet, Montana saw his horse lying only a few steps away. The scavengers had been at work, but, with a feast easily available, they had left him alone, sensing that he was not yet dead.

The herd was now only a distant blot against the horizon, except for such as had fallen, unable to rise again. The plain was pockmarked with them.

Cindy set him straight concerning their presence. The wagon which she had ordered had been far slower in arriving than promised, and when it had finally come, the men she had intended to send along with it, to help with the drive, had refused to embark upon so hazardous a journey. The risks to be encountered before the cattle could be marketed had seemed bad enough in any case. Then, as they pointed out, the herd was already far up the trail, and a lone wagon might never overtake them.

Since the others refused, Cynthia herself had set out, accompanied by Mandy – two lone women, their resolution putting to shame the timidity of the men. But even when challenged by such an example, the men had not changed their minds.

The trail left by the herd was easy to follow, but, remembering the not so empty wilderness which they had set out to traverse, Montana was appalled. But they were there, passing lightly over the hardships and terrors. They had brought the promised supplies, goods vital to the success of the drive.

The women had reached the northernmost of the chain of lakes when the first stragglers from the turned-about herd had commenced coming in. Shocked by the appearance of the cattle, the waterless horror of the dry country, they had lost no time in filling every available container with water, then coming on to do anything possible. They had succored three others of the crew, who might not have made it back but for their assistance. Hearing that Montana was one of the remaining quartet, hope had almost given way to despair before they had sighted one more bevy of buzzards, which had led them to him.

Mandy had not exaggerated. Except for their coming, he would not have survived.

He drank again, then ate, trying to remember when he'd had his last previous meal. By then, still wobbly but improving, he was ready to go. He pulled the saddle from his dead horse, loaded it into the wagon, and they headed for the lake.

The big team, fresh and well watered, stepped out briskly. They began to overtake more stragglers, but part of the herd had made it to the water ahead of them. Henson, meeting the wagon, expressed the common amazement.

"Live and learn," he said. "I've heard stories about dry drives an' all, and never quite believed them. And what's happenin' now is more surprising than all the rest. In the middle of that dry stretch, when the water we looked for wan't there, I didn't think that any of the critters could survive, or keep going till they made it back. Even if they did, I sure figured they'd founder, from drinkin' too much once they got to water. But you know, they've got as much sense as humans – maybe more –"

The cattle continued to come in, straggling

in small segments – all the way from one to half a hundred. Heads raised when they smelled the water from far off, and their pace quickened, though not by much. There was no real spurt of energy left in dried-out skeletons; only the thirst, the will to keep on to water. Reaching the wide, shallow lake, they waded out, often until nearly submerged.

"And then they stand and soak – but they go mighty slow on drinkin'," Henson added unbelievingly. "Sometimes they hardly touch a drop for minutes; just soak it in through their hides. And that's a mighty pleasant sensation, when you're as dirty and dried up as I was. I soaked, too, for better'n an hour after I got here. Then they drink, a little at a time. Yeah, they sure show more sense than I ever expected."

Most of the crew, rested and restored, were working the herd, riding back to round up stragglers, to keep them on the move for the last vital stretch. It was a slow process, but time was of no particular consequence.

Once the dogies had soaked and slaked their thirst by easy stages, they climbed back to dry ground, to lie down and sleep as though drugged. Awakening, they would drink again, then spread out to graze.

Thinking back to the desperate ordeal, it was hard to believe, but most of the herd
90

was surviving. The losses, for so big a herd, had remained nominal. Just as surprising, not a man had been lost. Montana had come the closest, having driven himself relentlessly until, like his horse, the limit had been reached.

Half a dozen horses had died. But over all it had been a weeding out of the weak and the stragglers. Sight was returning to the cattle with rest and water. They would soon be as ready as before.

Montana despatched Curley to check on the wagons up ahead and the cook and his helper. He made the round trip in a couple of days, reporting back that Grady was waiting for them to catch up.

All at once there was a different feel to the air, a portent of change. Mulroney voiced it, casting a knowing eye at a lowering dawn – to a sky no longer bright and hot, but cloudy.

"Drought's fixing to break," he observed. "My guess is that there'll be rain before night – and a lot of it."

With rain, they could resume the march, and the wide dry country would no longer be a hazard. But now they were faced with another problem, one which disturbed Montana more than he liked to admit. What was to be done about Cindy and Mandy?

He owed his life to them, and they had displayed more courage and resolution than some of the men. But for women to take part in a trail drive was unheard of, particularly with such perils as would be attendant upon this one. The dangers which he had anticipated were still to be met. Under the best of conditions, the country called The Nations, the strip of territory ruled by the renegades, lying between them and the market in Missouri, was not country for a woman.

On the other hand, having delivered the wagon as promised, Cindy and Mandy were there, and they could not go back. To send them on the back trail alone was unthinkable. They had been lucky coming north, but their luck should not be pressed too far. Nor could he spare an escort of several men to see them back to the San Saba. Even now they were short-handed.

Cindy brought up the matter over the dying campfire. The storm still held off, dragging its heels beyond the time which Mulroney had estimated, but the clouds had drawn in as the day ended. Now they made a solid rim of the night. The feel of rain, all the terrors of darkness, of the wide wasteland ahead, seemed crouched just beyond the flickering coals.

"Mandy and I will drive our wagon and do the cooking for all of you once we catch up with Grady," Cindy said. "That will free him and the cookee to ride. That way, we won't be a burden."

"It's not as a burden that I've been thinking of you," Montana assured her, "especially after what you've done. But I hardly know what to say, with a trail of the sort that lies ahead –"

"Meaning that it is no place for women," Cindy finished for him. "I agree, Bill. When it comes to that, it is no place for anyone, but the rest of you are going – and what else is there to do? Anyhow, a part of this herd belongs to me, and so they are in some measure my responsibility. If trouble comes, I can ride as fast and far as any man, and shoot as straight."

"I don't doubt any of that," Montana agreed. "But, entirely aside from outside trouble –" He shrugged, then made a gesture in admission of defeat. "Some of the men aren't going to like having you along. But as you say, what else is there to do?"

Cindy smiled and nodded. There was a dimple at the corner of her mouth, and a loose tendril of hair curled on the cheek above, mute testimony to the fact that she was a woman. But she was not of the pattern of those cherished, half-helpless ladies of the Southland of even a decade before. As she had demonstrated, she belonged to the category of comrades who across the ages had stood beside their men-folk to fight off whatever perils might threaten; who rocked the cradle, but also grasped a rifle or a plow.

When it came to that, plenty of pampered women, both South and North, had surprised their men-folk, if not themselves, as hardships and dangers had swept away the old order. They had met the challenge with a courage to match that of their ancestors.

Cynthia understood the hazards, probably as well as anyone, but she was undeterred. Montana bowed gravely, but his pulse quickened.

"I'll be proud to have you along," he admitted.

11

Making a decision was fairly simple, but it did not insure a desired result. What must inevitably lie ahead hung in Montana's mind like a dark cloud, piling and twisting.

His initial problems were not long in materializing. Some of the crew had overheard at least snatches of his conversation with Cindy, and the news spread like flame in

94

dry grass. The reaction was almost as fast. Henson and Curley came up as Montana was throwing a saddle on a pony, preparatory to taking a final look at the herd before rolling in his blanket. Other shadowy figures lurked in the background.

"What's this I hear, Abbott, about takin' the women along with us?" Henson's tone was abrupt. "Are you plumb crazy?"

"Can you think of a better solution?" Montana countered.

"Who couldn't? Send 'em back, of course. You know what things will be like, and the farther up the trail we go, the worse they'll get. Such country's no place for women."

"I agree," Montana said wearily, and his refusal to argue left them at a loss. "But we can't send them back, by themselves and on horseback to sleep in the open. We can't spare enough men to escort them all the way to the San Saba. And we can't leave them here. So what else is there, Sam? You were about to say that you wouldn't agree, but tell me what else there is? Would you still send them back?"

Henson chewed doggedly at the ragged end of his mustache, and his ready answer of a minute before was not articulated. Curley was more adamant.

"It's not that simple," he protested

95

doggedly. "I'm not against women, you understand, and they've sure helped us out, bringin' the wagon and all. But we've trouble now, and it can grow one heck of a lot worse. Some of the boys say they won't go, not with women along."

Montana put a foot in the stirrup, swung up, then leaned from the saddle. His voice was as soft as water slipping along under ice, and just as chill.

"Don't let me hear any more such talk, Curley, from you or anyone," he warned. "You had a choice of staying to rot along the San Saba, or coming on this drive. You made it. Now we're on our way, and I'm trail boss. I give the orders, and they'll be obeyed. It's not that I want to show my authority, or to get tough, but because from now on it's a matter of life and death."

He waited, looking down, but there was no further argument. After a minute he headed into the night, welcoming the feel of storm. After threatening all through the day it hit, a roaring blast of rain out of sudden clotting blackness. Then the darkness was slashed by crimson swords which tore the night to tatters, ripping with shattering savagery. The darkness closed in again, only to explode anew.

As the deluge slapped at him, there came

a vast, concerted grunt as the herd surged to their feet, then the hammering of hoofs on hard-packed earth as thousands of animals plunged in unreasoning terror. Here was the madness of stampede.

A week before, he'd known the futility of total helplessness in the blaze of the sun, the torment of thirst which closed the throat and parched a man's lungs inside his body. This was different, yet in some respects strangely the same. Here was cool wetness and a completely different sort of emergency. But the cattle were up and running; even if the horsemen could see to act, nothing could stem or turn so wild a sweep. Watered, rested, grown impatient after days of idleness, the cattle were in a mood to run.

Before the night was over they could scatter so that another week would hardly suffice to round them up again. And luck would be as necessary as hard work. Montana wondered if this drive was jinxed, doomed to failure.

Here was one of the big hazards of any drive. But the other known dangers, perils for which he had been prepared, were all still ahead. It was the things he'd not expected or been able to foresee which kept hitting them.

Ordinarily, men could see and work to control a stampede; there was a tried pattern at such times, to swing the leaders, set the whole herd to milling. Here such hard-won knowledge was useless, impossible to apply. Never had he ridden in more utter darkness. Each flash of lightning seemed to sear the eyelids, leaving blindness in its wake.

His horse was running, but it was movement inspired by panic, without plan or purpose. Then the thunder and lightning stopped as suddenly as it had begun, though the rain continued, along with the impenetrable dark.

Above the beat of the storm there came another sound unrecognizable at first, then hardly to be mistaken. It was like the mad threshing of a great sea monster.

Montana pulled his horse to a trembling stop. Ears alone were useful. The turmoil took on a different quality, slackening, and in the threshing and churning there seemed a quality of bewilderment. No longer was there the pounding of hard-running hoofs, though they had not receded in the distance. The end of the run had been as sudden as its start.

Off to the south appeared a tear in the clouds, a jagged break through which faint starshine muted the total quality of the night. The gap widened as the rain slackened; then a thin mist of moon silvered the expanse of the lake. The normally placid pond was now churned and troubled as if by an avenging angel. There was light enough to confirm what Montana's ears had already told him, to verify one more shift of luck.

Actually, what had happened was simple enough, a normal result, given the set of circumstances. The running herd, stampeding without purpose, running blindly through the night, had plunged straight into the lake. For the first time in days, a grin lifted Montana's mustache, as he pictured the bewilderment of bovine minds at finding themselves in such a predicament. Certainly it was the last thing for which they had been prepared.

The lake had received the herd, somewhat as it had done some days before, this time as a plunging mass instead of slowly venturing individuals. It was not deep enough to be a hazard, and the rocky bottom was solid. Only at a few spots was the depth great enough to be over the head of a steer.

Halted now in the water, the tear of lightning and the blasting thunder over with, they cooled off in a hurry. Call it chance or luck, in any case disaster had been averted.

Remembering their long thirst, the delicious quality of the water as they had soaked, the animals were in no hurry to get back out. They did so gradually, bedding down, content, pleased with the steady quality of the rain. The breaks in the clouds, after revealing the sight, had repaired themselves. Its first gusty fury vented, the storm continued on a quieter note.

Morning showed no sign of a let-up. The dust of drought had been transmuted to mud; the searing quality of summer was supplanted by spring, deliciously cool.

Morning found everyone in high good humor at the long awaited change in the weather. The feeling was heightened as they understood just how lucky they had been. The solid edge of the plunging mass of longhorns had missed the camp by no more than a stone's throw. By veering only a little, the herd might have smashed across it, a juggernaut which would have trampled men and horses, even wagons.

In the face of such fortune, there was no complaining about the wet and restless night, or the new problems which the storm imposed. Dry wood had been gathered as the storm threatened and had been stored under the wagons. Cindy and Mandy managed a hot breakfast for everyone.

"And that's mighty tasty grub, ma'am," Curley said generously. "Don't know when I've et fodder to compare with it."

The wagon swung off, Cindy driving, Mandy's ample figure sagging her side of the seat. The herd lined out behind. The sixty miles which had been a baking hell would present no problems aside from mud and the discomfort of the rain. They could even find enjoyment in that sort of trouble.

They picked up the other wagons in due course, and now the land was less wild, more pleasant under a temperate sun. The backlash of war had not quite swept away the pioneering of earlier decades. Here and there a ranch was still inhabited. As along the San Saba, it was more an existence than a living, but there was one pleasing difference. This country was not worth the attention of the carpetbaggers and if a man starved, he could do so with a measure of dignity.

Encountering some settlers, they received news, hardly realizing that they were also making it. Theirs was the first herd to venture toward Missouri from the heartland of Texas for a considerable spell. The hardships encountered by prior drives, the disasters which had stopped them short of their goal, had discouraged even the stout-hearted. For someone to try again was noteworthy.

A white-bearded patriarch combed his whiskers with his fingers, eying Montana with doubt and uneasy admiration.

"So you're Abbott," he observed. "We've heard a considerable bit about you – no offense intended, Cap'n. And I reckon if anybody can get a herd through, it'll be you."

He said no more, seeming all at once to realize that perhaps he already had been too loose-tongued. Others at the ranch eyed them oddly, but were even less communicative. There was no hostility, but the settlers seemed relieved that the herd was passing through with as little delay as possible.

"They look at you like you was a cross between the devil and a trail-bustin' pioneer," Sam Henson observed. "You must have made quite a reputation for yourself in Gin'ral Lee's army, Cap'n – probably more'n we ever got word of, way off like we were."

"Sure, man, and it was not only while he was soldiering," Mulroney spoke up, his smile bland. " 'Tis a name known along the Border – and it's lucky we are to have such a man in charge!"

Montana made no reply, eying Mulroney somewhat askance. He still wore the gold-mounted guns of a dead man, and with them he had inherited their late owner's reputation, which he could neither explain, disclaim or take credit for. But that reputation was proving an asset. Because of it, the others were more inclined to follow, to credit him with luck – luck which had brought them this far intact.

What it might be like from here on

remained to be discovered. An asset could quickly become a liability.

They crossed the Leon, the Brazos, and finally the Red, none of the streams presenting serious problems. The weather continued pleasant, no longer too hot or too dry, as fine as could be hoped for at that season of the year. There was grass in abundance, water enough, no open hostility, no real problems. It was almost too good to be true.

So was the behavior of the crew, especially as concerned Cindy. A part of that might be attributed to Mandy, looming like a watchful duenna, but a larger amount of the credit went to Montana, whose authority was now beyond dispute. He was fair, and no one questioned what he said; or, even more important what he left unsaid.

He observed that Mulroney grew more alert and watchful, as though entering familiar but risky territory.

"A word to the wise," Mulroney observed, where all might hear. "From here on, this is what we might call Border country – and the word has been whispered like a shout. Along the Border, the name of Abbott is as well known as along the San Saba – and 'tis a foolish or foolhardy man who asks questions."

No one did ask the questions which cried

out for answers. Only Sam Henson added a caution as well.

"A woman can make or break a man," he told the crew bluntly, out and well away from the wagons. "And that goes for all women, whether a sweetheart or wife or a termagant, as the case may be. Thus far everyone has kept certain things in mind and behaved well, but from here on, every man has got to consider the women as our collective responsibility. We have to see that nothing happens to them – from any source. Havin' them along helps to keep us civilized, which any bunch of men can stand.

"I reckon I've made myself plain. I'll add just this much. Abbott is concerned about getting this drive through, cattle, men and women alike. He's fair and square. But I'm only telling you what you already know when I remind you that he'd kill anybody that stepped out of line, and in that, I'm backin' him all the way."

Beyond the Red they were out of Texas, and the half-tamed land was a memory. Now came The Nations, a different stretch from that which Montana had crossed in swift and stealthy fashion. Here was as wild a stretch of country as even the most lawless man might seek. Any one man's knowledge of such territory must of necessity be limited. Few had ventured along these wastes and returned to tell what they had found.

Only one good thing could be said for it, and that was a matter of degree. Most of the native inhabitants were less savage than the later arrivals of paler skin who haunted the dreaded Border, short of where civilization was again to be found.

They reached a last outpost, a tiny settlement with a store sufficiently stocked to enable them to replenish the wagons. Montana reflected that the last of his hoard of gold had been put to excellent use.

Montana rode at once loose and tight-reined – loose on whatever horse he bestrode, tight within himself. Realizing the increasing pleasure which he found in Cindy's company, how he had come to watch for her smile or listen to the gaiety of her laugh, he understood anew the crowding loneliness of the long trail.

He was a long day's ride ahead of the wagons, scouting with increasing wariness. And here, under the stars, he could face the truth, admit it to himself. Cynthia was like that brighter star, hung out with all the others in the sky, yet above and beyond them all.

He understood, at least in part, why Cindy was making this trip, facing its hazards. It was not alone because of the poverty along the San

Saba, the needs of her own spread. There was Tom, still too weak from a long illness to come himself –

Montana had seen the way the two had looked at one another, the softness in her eyes when she had spoken his name. That was fine, and one more thing to remember.

He smothered his campfire, then was preparing, with a soldier's instinct, to draw away and sleep well back from where the fire had burned, when he heard a sound. Someone was coming, a vague shadow in the night. Here in The Nations, any visitor was likely to be an enemy.

There seemed to be only one rider. Montana stared in an amazement which grew to disbelief as the horse assumed form and substance, and he saw the rider. Not an Indian, but white. And not a man, but a woman. And not merely a woman, but, seen more closely, a creature breath-takingly lovely under the glow of the summer stars.

12

She came on, directly toward the now blackened campfire, pulling up with the air of one who had reached an intended destination. Her voice was melodic, like the fluting of a night bird.

"A pleasant good evening to you, sir. I bid you welcome to the Border."

Montana stared, forced to look upward, his amazement increasing. By contrast with hair which seemed as black as the surrounding shadows, her face was surprisingly fair, as though wind and sun had touched it softly, as lightly as the caress of the moon. Her eyes were equally deep, her lips parted in question. Before he could reply, she spoke again.

"You may help me down if you will."

Bemused, he obeyed, reaching to assist her, and the next moment she was in his arms, her full weight momentarily against him, her breath soft on his face. It had been a long while, well before the war, since he'd detected the subtle fragrance of such perfume; such costly cosmetics had become, for most women, only a remembered luxury. With Cindy, there was a fresh, natural cleanness like the prairie wind, but it was not perfume. Here, at the rim of The Nations, he encountered a drift of fragrance as intoxicating as heady wine.

She sighed as he set her on her feet, and took a backward step. He caught a gleam of what might have been amusement before her long lashes dropped.

"Thank you, sir. I am somewhat stiff from being long in the saddle."

Immediately belying that assertion, she swung with a supple grace, glancing around, then looked back at him. Her tone was faintly mocking.

"I fear that I have completely discomposed you," she observed. "Or are you always so silent?"

"I haven't been accused of it before," he returned. "But I confess to being bewildered. I had no idea that there would be any woman, anywhere in this territory – and certainly no one such as you."

"You make amends quite nicely." She smiled, and with the smile a dimple came and went in her cheek. "Why don't we sit and talk, become better acquainted? It's so lovely an evening."

Allowing her horse to graze as it wished, she spread her skirts and seated herself on the grass. The gesture was not lost on Montana, increasingly surprised that, riding here, she would wear a riding skirt, such as would be appropriate in the settled country east of the river. At her gesture, he took a place nearby, his senses alert. Here was no ordinary woman. He was conscious of her charm, of her power to attract.

Who she was and where she had come from were no more important than that she had clearly come there to see him, riding alone and unannounced. Clearly, she had known about him, and his movements had been watched.

"It is a nice evening," he agreed. "Folks always consider the weather a safe topic for conversation. But I don't believe that it interests either of us. Am I to suppose that you live around here, and are just out for a short ride?"

Her laugh was both pleased and amused.

"As I had been led to suppose, you are a man of parts, Captain. It is Captain Abbott, isn't it? Coincidences do happen. I'm sure that we can find much besides the weather to talk about. In fact, I think we'll get on very well together."

Montana was watching the outer rim of the darkness, his ears strained for some other betraying sound. But there was nothing to hear or see.

"Relax, Captain," she murmured, and amusement rippled in her laughter. "I'm alone. I spent a good part of the afternoon watching you, and decided that we should become better acquainted. You've been doing a good job with your scouting, I'm sure. As of the present, you have nothing to worry about. Such Indians as there are in this section will remain well away from your herd while you are under my protection."

She made the statement without a change of inflection, rendering it doubly challenging and provocative. The words carried a claim which verged on the incredible if not the impossible. Montana was as wary as a wolf scenting a trap. He waited expectantly for her to go on, and faint impatience as well as a malicious overtone were in her next words.

"You are a fortunate man, Captain – and more lucky than you may realize. And I am in your debt."

"Ma'am, if you're trying to tangle me in a spiderweb of words, you're sure managing," he confessed.

Her laugh rippled again on a pleased note, and she moved a little closer.

"But does not every woman seek to do that with a man she likes?" He was certain that she was mocking him, but not yet sure of her purpose. "I have heard much about you, so that I was sure that I would like you. And I do."

His blood was racing, as she intended that it should, as much from the provocative quality of her words as from her tantalizing nearness. This was unbelievable, something which could not be happening, yet it was. Montana responded with a suddenness which appeared impetuous, but his mind was as cold and calculating as the one with which he sparred. She had come there to play games. Well, he could play, too. He reached out, drawing her close, then kissed her hard.

Her gasp was one of pure surprise, but her response was swift and pleased. Her arms tightened in turn, and her lips were eager.

It came to him that this could be a risky game, even for a man as hard-headed as himself. He drew back, aware that he was more deeply stirred than he had counted on. Her eyes laughed at him.

"Bravo, Captain! Now I know that I like you! Your coming is a dividend beyond what I had expected."

"I guess I could say the same thing," he returned, covering an ever sharper sense of caution. Where would this sparring lead or end? He was strongly tempted to repeat the performance, but dared not. It would be too hard to keep his head.

"You are Captain Abbott," she said, "first a Confederate officer, then a Yankee recruit. You have a reputation for luck – as a man who makes his own. I think that it is a part of both. Otherwise, when you were set upon, in your sleep, knocked senseless and your clothes taken, you would have been killed, as it was intended you should be. Yet he who dealt so treacherously with you died instead, while you lived."

Montana listened in growing surprise. "You seem to know a lot about that."

"Of course. And why not? I make it my business to know. Captain Abbott was desperate, a frightened man, a once brave man who had become a coward. He picked upon you largely by chance, probably not knowing who you were, or guessing that your name and rank were the same. But I doubt that it would have made any difference, even had he known. He was desperate. Who should know better than I, who was his wife?"

So his guess, wild as it had seemed, was correct. Abbott of the Border! And now other memories were stirring, some from far back, buried among the strife and vagaries of war – of another Abbott, serving in the far-flung armies of the Confederacy, an officer who had become almost a legendary figure during those first years of war. His reputation for skill and daring at least matched Montana's.

Most of the time there had been at least a thousand miles between them, and reports had been more like rumors. Then something had gone wrong with this other Captain Abbott, a tale never fully told, only whispered. He had moved, whether from choice or necessity, to engage in Border war – in Kansas, Missouri, The Nations. He had become one of that shadowy company of raiders, feared and hated almost as much by one side as the other.

Apparently he had ended up in disfavor with his superiors and with the Confederacy. The dislike must have been mutual. In it would undoubtedly have been a residue of bitterness. His new stature, as a leader of renegades, would hardly compensate for what had been lost; especially to a man who had been reared a gentleman.

There was much of the story which Montana did not know, but now he had heard enough to clear up a number of minor mysteries. It had been this other Abbott, then, who had fled the Border country where once he had been all but supreme. Clearly he had tried to escape enemies bent on his destruction. This woman, as fair in appearance as the moon riding high overhead, who confessed to being his wife, had made that clear. It was doubly ironic, as was her description of a once brave man who had become a coward!

Desperate, his namesake had been driven to the expedient of assaulting a sleeping man, trading clothes with him, with the hope that, free of the betraying uniform in which he had fled, he might elude those who hunted him.

It hadn't worked out that way. Whether the renegade had hoped or intended that the killers might mistake the wearer of the officer's outfit, and believe their mission was accomplished, was pure speculation. The ruse had not worked.

For himself, the uniform had been good luck rather than bad – but the end was not yet. Montana felt as though a chill wind blew, though the night remained warm. This woman, in calmly revealing that she had been the wife of Abbott of the Border, was admitting at least a degree of complicity in the murder of her husband. He had been hunted to his death.

What lay back of it all was of no overriding importance, save that it had happened. His impulse as regarded the spider had been prophetic. Montana hid a shiver, recalling how the black widow made a practice of dining on her mate.

She was bewitchingly beautiful, and she had demonstrated no hesitation in using her charm to attain her own ends. Widowed, she seemed pleased rather than grieved.

Just as surely, the man or men dispatched to hound the other Abbott to his death had returned and reported. Their account would not only have dealt with the dead man, but must have included the man who had succeeded to his uniform, and who by coincidence had the same name. She knew all about Montana Abbott and the drive he was rodding toward Missouri.

Such Indians as lurk – no, her words had been, *as there are in this section will remain well away from your herd while you are under my protection!*

She had dropped the remark with apparent lightness, but he had a hunch that it might be the truth rather than a boast. His own situation could take some pondering.

Abbott of the Border had been almost a legendary figure. Now, having worn his uniform, with the coincidence of circumstance and the name, some of that reputation had brushed off on him. Most people were probably unaware of the difference, that one was dead, and that they were two different men.

This other Captain Abbott had been brave

to the point of recklessness, an officer so skilled that his luck had become a byword in the Army. It must have been a devastating experience which could have changed him into a coward, afraid, fleeing for his life, despised by such a woman.

There, perhaps, was the key. This woman was outwardly soft and lovely, deeply desirable. But she had virtually admitted to being savage and relentless. She must have been a powerful factor in her husband's rise, as she had been in his downfall. A woman could make or break a man. In this case she apparently had done both. Once she had loved him. Later, just as clearly, she had tired of him.

Again, the reasons were not important. It was sufficient that these things had happened, that she had become so ruthless and powerful a figure among the lawless legion that Abbott had been compelled to flee, a broken man. Probably the process had been long, tortuous and involved; the result was what counted. That had been a bullet from an ambush, an unmarked grave.

Montana shivered. The movement was involuntary, beyond his control. She was quick to observe, shrewd in understanding. Her smile held a hint of mockery coupled with reassurance.

"So now you understand, and you are dismayed? But don't be frightened, Captain Abbott. You are much too brave, too fortunate a man, to have ground for apprehension, particularly of me."

He waited, half believing her despite what he knew, certain that he must remain wary. He was sure that she meant what she said, but that was hardly reassuring. A thought flashed through his mind, a remark made long years before by his father. At the time, he had been discussing religious beliefs, and had derided the notion that Satan walked about with hoofs and horns.

"I figure he wouldn't do it, not a shrewd old devil like him," he'd scoffed. "That way, even a fool would recognize him for what he was. No, you'd find him in the guise of a mighty fine, pleasant gentleman, as charming as all get-out. Or maybe in the form of a beautiful woman."

This woman was beautiful, but she had tired of Abbott of the Border. Perhaps, realizing her own powers, she had aspired to complete control along the frontier, jealous of sharing such leadership even with her husband. Whatever the reasons, she had dominated.

Now she was intrigued by this fresh chain of events, which at least in their inception had hardly been of her making. There was the name, Abbott, and, not to be overlooked, the size and value of the big herd. She was ready and eager for a new plaything. Wryly, Montana recognized that, on close inspection, he apparently filled the bill.

"I'm afraid I'm a bit confused," Montana confessed. "Some of this kind of jars me."

"Or perhaps it is that *I* rock you a little?" she suggested tantalizingly. "But was it not pleasant, Captain? I found it so."

"I certainly didn't find it unpleasant," he admitted, and did not add that the distasteful part had come with better understanding. Again her laugh purred.

"I like you, Montana," she confessed. "You have such audacity – and I like that in a man. Also a reckless courage, to set out to take a herd through, where others have failed and died. But, Montana, with me on your side, you just might succeed – all the way."

Her words were at once an invitation and a promise, but he made no reply. She jumped to her feet, as light and graceful as a vixen, catching up her horse and going into the saddle in a single flowing movement. From there she looked down, then was gone in a quick flurry of hoofs. But an added promise floated back.

"Together, my dear Captain, we can do

anything! Remember that. We will meet again."

13

Montana stared into the darkness, which had swallowed the receding figure of Mrs. Abbott. Again the night wind blew cold. Her words had been intended as a promise, filled with reassurance. Still, they were disturbingly like a threat.

The whole episode was strange, bordering on the eerie. And that was in keeping with this country, the wild Border. The Nations had a growing reputation as an evil, chilling land. Out of it had ridden this woman, warm, lovely to look at, riding alone and unattended – as if such a place were home!

Or did she ride alone? A sound brought him quickly about, one of the golden guns in his hand. Knowingly or otherwise, she had not ridden entirely by herself.

A shadowy figure paused, facing the leveled revolver like a cornered animal. The light was a little brighter as the moon attained its full splendor, affording Montana a good target. The fellow had been crouching there, watching and listening, then had stumbled when turning to creep away.

"All right," Montana said tightly. "Keep your hands up and don't try to run. Now, what's the idea?"

The skulker approached, moving reluctantly, a shambling, gawky figure. Montana mistook him for a boy, then changed his mind. He was at once frightened yet defiant.

"I reckon I got a right to watch out for her," he mumbled. "A woman like her, riding alone after dark in country like this – it's risky business, even for her."

Montana understood and felt sorry for the kid. Youthful enough to cling to ideals, even in such an environment, he was in love with her, hopelessly infatuated. Undoubtedly he realized the hopelessness of his passion. She was a woman who would treat him kindly, but that was much as she might toss a bone to a hound, then slap it sharply if it growled over the offering.

But common sense, or even an awareness of the realities, had little to do with a man's emotions, especially at such an age. Montana was all too aware of that. The kid's was the blind, faithful loyalty of the hound, seeking in return no more than an occasional kind word or a pat on the head.

"I expect you're right about that," Montana conceded. "But I doubt that she'd like it if she knew you'd been following her."

"She'd kill me," the boy admitted humbly. "Just the same, none of us like her doing things alone, taking all sorts of chances."

"None of us?" Montana repeated.

"None of your business –" The snarl changed to a defeated hopelessness. "Oh, what's the difference? Other people call us outlaws. And I suppose we are."

Montana had the picture, and it was much as he'd expected. Captain Abbott had relinquished his honor and integrity somewhere along the way – quite possibly the final step had come from the bitterness of defeat. Yet long before that he had become a renegade, setting his hand against not only the conquerors of his southland, but against all men. That he might perhaps have repented of such a choice after it was too late was beside the point. His name and fame, along with his qualities of leadership, had made him a power along the Border.

Now he was dead, but his lobo pack was very much alive. And his wife had become their leader! Well, stranger things had happened. Such a woman, using her wiles along with her beauty, might very well attain domination even over so ruthless an outfit. The boy's next remark seemed to confirm that.

"Generally she pretends to listen when we give an opinion, but usually that's as far as it goes. She's headstrong, and likes to do things her way."

"She must do a pretty good job, if the rest of you follow her," Montana suggested.

The kid scuffed a boot toe in the dirt.

"Yeah, she manages right good. There ain't hardly a man along the Border that wouldn't follow her to hell and back if she asked him to. That's why her word's law with us. There's something about her – well, you saw for yourself." His tone turned bitter. "I don't know why you should be so lucky, or what she sees in you."

Montana might have explained, but it would have been a waste of breath. Such a woman, eager for power and excitement, was rarely content with a taste. Having attained success beyond her wildest dreams, she craved new thrills, fresh conquests. And he offered both an opportunity and a challenge. That he might be cast aside as carelessly as the other Abbott, once she tired of the game, made no difference at the moment.

"Luck?" Montana picked out the word and allowed it to hang in the air.

"That's what I said," the kid returned

122

resentfully. "I saw and heard. And if she wants you, that's all right with me. Whatever she wants is what I want." His clearly was a faithful but blind devotion; he realized that he could never do more than worship from afar. "And if you've any sense, you'll take her love and treat her nice. You're the first man the Border Witch has really liked since she broke up with *him*."

The Border Witch! Montana repeated the name, staring at the place where the kid had slipped away in the darkness. He might have guessed. It was an appellation almost if not quite as well known as Abbott's, and at least as frightening. There were many whispered reports, rumors which he'd never quite credited, of a woman whose word and whim were as blinding as law –

Clearly, the tales emanating from this range of wolves had some basis in fact. And he was in a fair way to discover how much was truth, how much imagination.

Certain things he did know. Mrs. Abbott exercised authority, doing pretty much as she pleased. More to the point, she seemed to have fixed on him as the current object of her affections. There were wild and intriguing stories concerning him, and she would have heard perhaps distorted versions about the manner in which he had acquired the uniform and the brace of gold-mounted guns. And there was the luck which had saved him from a bullet in the back – .

But luck could take strange twists. Montana's concept of a witch certainly did not fit this woman. She was young, beautiful and desirable. She was also probably as dangerous and unpredictable as a blind rattlesnake. Those might be deemed witch-like attributes, or merely those of a spoiled woman, accustomed to having her own way.

As a woman, she would be satisfied with nothing less than all that a man had to give. Certainly she would accept no halfway commitment.

Here were opportunities as well as risks. If he took what she had said at face value, and was willing to take what she offered, there would be a good chance of getting the trail herd through to Missouri. Her lobo pack might resent such favoritism, and especially the loss of the booty. But she would probably be generous, and powerful enough to enforce her will.

Such a choice deserved serious consideration, not so much for his own sake as for the sake of the others who were involved – Sam Henson, Cindy Cartright –

He had counted on a long and hard trail,

requiring luck as well as hard fighting. What he had not foreseen were the complications which kept developing.

If the herd could reach Missouri and be sold for a good price, then would come the equally tough problem of getting back to Texas with the proceeds. On such matters depended the future of the others, and to a considerable measure, the poverty or prosperity of the country drained by the San Saba.

Should he scorn the proffered favors of the Border Witch, the dangers would be multiplied. Others had tried, encountering disaster, torture and death. For Cindy, it could be even worse.

But a free passage north would certainly be no guarantee of a safe-conduct south again with the spoils –

A night of pondering, with very little sleep, only added to his perplexity. He was sweating as he rode the next day, though a cool breeze stirred the crest of the grasses. If this was luck –

I could do with less, or a lot more. He groaned, and wondered grimly what the next act might be, when it would unfold. Sooner or later, he would have to make a choice. Whichever way he decided could easily be wrong, perhaps tragic. And the hard part was that much of it was out of his hands.

They had to keep going, for it was impossible to turn back.

"And I thought a dry drive was about the worst thing that could happen," he muttered. "It would have been easier to starve in Texas!"

The sun was high when Montana sighted the herd, the strung-out line of animals moving steadily north. This was another hot day, the warmest since that stretch of weather beyond the lakes. There was no lack of water here, no suffering from shortages, but Grady for one was finding it miserable. Fair of skin, he belonged to that group who refuse to tan, burning instead. He had confessed he became a cook, in preference to being a cowboy, because such a job offered more shelter from the sun.

The trio of wagons rumbled in advance of the herd, pitching and dipping, jouncing, the sun reflecting back from the stained but still glaring canvas tops. They were in more brushy country now, fringing the ravines which ran back like probing fingers from the valley. Montana watched uneasily. There had been no trouble, no threat of attack; still, this was perfect range for ambush.

As if in line with his thoughts, a heavy gun blast slammed harshly against the silence, then echoed and re-echoed along the gulches.

126

Like puppets jerked by strings, horsemen spilled from coulee mouths on opposite sides, converging on the wagons.

The lead wagon was in trouble, the initial shot having found a target. Montana saw the figure on the seat lurch forward, out from under the scant shade afforded by the canvas top; a sunbonneted figure, who slumped against the corner of the wagon box. She settled down in the seat, losing the reins from fingers gone lax.

The startled team were quick to sense that trouble had struck, leaving them with no control, no strong hand to guide and reassure them. They broke into a gallop, then checked savagely as another rifle bullet erupted from the same hidden source. It dropped the off horse as effectively as the first shot had felled the driver, and the remaining animal and wagon jolted to a stop.

Emotion choked Montana's throat like a surge of dust, a medley of dismay and rage. Unnoticed as he rode, he had an excellent view of the attack; its boldness was immediately clear. At least nine men were converging on the wagons, and the surprise had been all but complete. Then a tenth was revealed as the hidden rifleman rode into the open and pulled up to watch, long gun at the ready.

Surprise coursed in Montana along with

127

recognition. This was Watson, left wounded and defeated back at the San Saba. But whatever else might be said against him, Watson was not one to give up without a struggle. It had taken a long while before he was well enough to take up the chase, finally to catch up, with vengeance as his objective.

The attack had been well judged and timed. He had targeted Mandy with that first bullet, the big sunbonnet showing clearly. With the second shot the wagon had been anchored. Now his crew, sweeping in, were about to overwhelm the wagons and grab Cindy as a hostage. Once they had her, the rest would be easy.

The herd and the crew were a mile behind. With the wagons and supplies and Cindy in their hands, a fight would be one-sided. If it was persisted in, Cynthia would be sacrificed. Surrender would be the price for her life.

The rebel yell burst from Montana's throat, its wild paean Watson's first intimation that his plan was less than perfect, or that surprise could work both ways. For a moment he goggled, dismay blending with recognition. Then he brought up his rifle as Montana raced toward him at a full gallop. The long gun spilled its thunder for a third time, and that was the last as it missed. By then

128

Montana had closed to within six-gun range. He was wasting no bullets.

The sudden fusillade from the golden gun warned the attackers, jerking their heads around, spoiling their onslaught. Incredulous, they stared a moment, then tried to meet this menace, but the moment of bewilderment was overly long. Montana was making good use of both guns, emptying the first, then bringing the other into play. At point-blank range, the big forty-fives were devastating.

By now, other guns were joining in, working havoc among the disorganized attackers. The drivers of the other wagons were quick to seize the opportunity.

One man was still fighting back, as cool as though there had been no mishap. He was using his revolver as Montana closed the gap. Alabama Anson, devil-may-care as always. Fighting was his profession.

He watched Montana's approach with a derisive grin, then suddenly flinched and lost his grip on his gun. He steadied with an effort of will, trying with that emptied hand to clutch the saddle-horn, to save himself as he started to pitch sideways. His fingers closed, then loosened spasmodically. He fell, hitting heavily on one shoulder, held by a foot caught in the stirrup.

The cayuse was frantic with terror, but

training held it rooted to the spot as the reins dropped. Montana swept alongside, on his way to the wagons. Then the eyes of the dying man met his and locked, and Montana hesitated, then swung down. He loosened the twisted foot from the stirrup, allowing it to fall free. Alabama heaved a sigh of relief, and blood bubbled on his lips.

"Thanks," he gasped. "I didn't want to be dragged."

That it would hardly have mattered was clear. His eyes, gazing with a weak smile at Montana, glazed. The guns had fallen silent.

Montana, still on foot, moved ploddingly toward the wagons. His feet were reluctant.

Then his eyes lightened as he saw Cindy jumping from the second wagon, running to bury her head against his chest, to cling tightly.

"I thought it was you – there at the start," he managed, and Cindy lifted tear-bright eyes which held wonder and disbelief.

"And I thought I saw you go down," she confessed. "If you had, I'd have wanted to die, too."

14

It had been not quite a comedy of errors, since in that brief but bloody encounter tragedy raced side by side with death. Two or three of Watson's crew had fled successfully to the shelter of the gulches, but Watson and Alabama were dead, and even apart from them the price had been heavy.

There were two casualties for the trail crew. The horse was one. Grady was the other. He had cooked his last meal, short of the sky trails. Here again, chance and the mockery of luck had played its part.

A proud man, competent in the saddle, Grady had taken his place with the crew when Cindy and Mandy had caught up and taken over the cooking chores. Before that, despite the blistering sun, he'd fared reasonably well driving the chuck wagon, sheltered by its canvas from the sun.

"I had no idea how badly he was burning until last evening," Cindy explained chokingly. "But when he came in to supper, he was as red as though he'd been in a fire. By this morning, his face and arms were peeling. Mandy and I doctored him up as well as we

131

could, and Sam told him to drive a wagon and keep out of the sun. He was wearing one of Mandy's bonnets for added protection."

That Grady would submit to a bonnet showed how badly off he had been. Cindy and Mandy had been in the second wagon, neither visible nor on the seat. Mandy was ill, lying in the rear, and Cindy had been watching over her, making her as comfortable as possible, when the attack came.

Others of the crew had come up too late to join in the fight. Mulroney expressed the common feeling as he straightened from helping dig a common grave.

"You gave us no time, Captain, though like the other boys, I was doing my best. But what a grand view of a battle! Never have I beheld anything to match the way you handled those pretty little guns! Sure, and 'tis a broth of a fightin' man ye are!"

Coming from so redoubtable a warrior, it was a compliment, but Montana had long since discovered that the aftermath of battle was a bitter let-down. This time it was tempered by the knowledge of how much worse it might have been.

Cynthia had run to him and clung, but that was reaction from the attack. And a cactus flower, though of striking beauty, was encased in thorns.

132

The kid, the other evening, had let fall a remark before vanishing in the gloom. Mrs. Abbott, he'd informed Montana with bitterness and defiance, had had no eyes for any other man, no interest in anyone, since the death of her husband.

That had been his way of implying what might well be: that she could be capable of and would give love which, if responded to, would remain faithful and unswerving. Montana's lips twisted in mirthless humor.

The pain twisting his own heart was all that he needed to understand. A woman – be it Cindy, or her bewitchingly beautiful rival – could love deeply and passionately.

And I'm caught square in the middle, he reflected. The thought grew stronger when Henson joined him after the sober ordeal of supper.

"You run into any more trouble on up the trail?"

"Nothing that you could put a name to," Montana returned carefully. "It's an easy trail for a considerable way, with plenty of grass and water."

"No Injun sign?"

"If there are any 'Paches or Comanches hangin' around, they're keeping out of sight."

It sounded good. But there was trouble

133

ahead, and he could not even talk about it.

The next morning, Mandy again sagged on her side of the wagon seat, insisting that she could afford no time for ailing or puniness. That evening the two women served a tasty supper, having gone on ahead and found berry bushes, the limbs heavy with ripe fruit. Somehow they had contrived to make pies, hot and bubbly from the oven. Mulroney had knocked over a pronghorn, which made a welcome change from beef.

"Sure, and riding with a man of your luck, Montana, I'd have been a fool not to come on this drive." Mulroney yawned and grinned. "And you do have the luck!"

Montana eyed him sharply. It seemed an ordinary enough remark, but he was increasingly wary, more than usually distrustful, when such a tag was affixed to him.

He was taking his turn at riding night herd when a horseman came from the shadows, well distant from the fading remnants of the campfire, or the other cowboy who rode the circle.

This time he was not surprised at the woman's greeting. Her tone was soft and lazy.

"So you feast on fresh pie, cooked by a pretty pair of hands," she remarked. "You see, I watched from beyond that clump of brush. She is very pretty – almost as good-looking as I!"

The directness of that thrust was disconcerting. But Montana knew how to counter-attack.

"I like pretty women," he returned composedly, "particularly when they can cook."

"You are a man of parts, Montana, which is as I would have it." She nodded. "But why are women along on such a journey as this? That is not good."

"It wasn't planned that way," Montana admitted. "But she owns a part of the herd and one of the wagons. We needed the wagon, which hadn't come when we set out. When it did, the men who were to come with it got cold feet. So she and Mandy brought it. By the time they caught up, it was too late to turn back."

"How convenient. And you are not afraid to take women along on such a drive?"

"You seem to do very well in such country," he countered.

"So I do – but I am not quite like other women." Her eyes sparkled with challenge. "Have you not dreamed of our kiss – or wished for more?"

He'd realized all along that this was a

dangerous game, played for high stakes. The only possible chance for himself and the others lay in playing it boldly. He swung his horse alongside her, reaching, and she was flushed and eager. Then her horse danced and sidled, jerking its head as though in disapproval. As it pulled away, she spurred angrily. The startled cayuse bucked and reared, but was controlled with an iron hand.

"You are an impetuous man, Captain; perhaps a dangerous one." She surveyed him critically; then a smile played about the corners of her mouth. "That is the way I like it."

"So do I." His grin held its old devil-may-care quality. "Don't you think it's about time that you told me your name?"

"I was under the impression that you knew, since it is the same as yours. Mrs. Abbott."

"That I had gathered. But your first name?"

"My mother had romantic notions. I am Yolande."

Somehow the exotic quality of the name fitted her. He repeated it softly.

"Yolande. I like it."

"You are not too interested in this other woman, then?" she challenged. "This Cindy?"

"It has been a business proposition with
136

both of us. She inherited a ranch, after her father and brothers were killed. Like the rest of us, she needed a market."

Yolande's tone was half-bantering, half-serious.

"More and more I discover you to be a man of parts. A captain in both Armies – and of course I had assumed that made you a renegade at the least. Perhaps I have done you an injustice. So I will make you a promise, Montana. If your part of the herd is delivered and sold – as may happen, if you continue to treat me fairly in turn – then the rest of the cattle will be treated in the same way. You may find me a jealous woman, Montana, but I can also be generous."

Before he could reply, she swung her horse away and was gone in the deepening night with no further word or gesture. Montana stared after her, shaken. Here was no ordinary woman, though basically she was like all her sisters. Despite the lightness of her words, she was disturbed, and she was clearly jealous.

She was trying both the carrot and the stick. She had made him a promise, but a conditional one, holding a threat as well. Though she had set no terms, made no clear demand, he was not left in any doubt.

Once more the wind seemed to hold a chill, blowing out of the north. What he had suspected but hesitated to believe was now certain. Yolande was the Border Witch.

She belonged in that lawless stretch of country short of Missouri, short of the haven of the settled lands; that horror where the renegades controlled. She had ventured well south of her usual range, apparently out of curiosity concerning himself. But it seemed clear that she was widely respected and feared throughout The Nations; able not only to make promises, but to enforce them.

15

This was a roadless land through which they journeyed, the only trails those of wild game. During the war years, Texas had stagnated, her men drained to distant borders to do battle for a somewhat nebulous if glorious cause. A flurry of hope had followed the silencing of the guns, since there were markets hungry for beef, and the supply was more than adequate. Some men had lost no time in striking out with trail herds.

Only a few among all those who tried had

succeeded. They had encountered unexpected hazards, a horde of outlaws as devouring as locusts. All trails, like those in war, seemed to have a common goal of death. The effort to reach the markets had all but collapsed.

Such herds as had gotten this far had each followed its own route, and time and weather had pretty well erased such sign as they had made. So Montana kept going in a general direction, the sun his beacon, while the country grew increasingly rough and lonely. They were nearing the river called Canadian.

He had a hunch that the land was not so empty as it appeared, that other eyes watched their every move, but of this there was no outward sign. Captain Mulroney had proved his worth, especially as a scout. If there was any sign in earth or sky, his eyes picked it out as unfailingly as those of an eagle. So, instead of going himself, Montana sent him ahead to the river.

There was the hint of trouble when Mulroney failed to return as expected. Night gave way to a fresh blaze of sun, and there was still no sign of him as the herd lined out. Not until mid-afternoon, when the shores of the river were in sight, did he come loping back, a crimson welt alongside his neck.

"Arrow," he explained laconically. "Sure,

and the painted devils grow ambitious. They had me pinned down for a spell, before I contrived to slip away. And though I do say it myself, I kind of pulled a whizzer on them. I moved a bit to the side, till they lost track of where I might be, and then, when they got to jabberin', I joined in. It being too dark to tell the difference they mistook me for one of them."

"So you can speak Cherokee like a native?"

"If not that good, at least passin' well. I lived among them for a couple of years."

Mulroney did not elaborate. If there was a possibility of treachery in this, it seemed removed by the arrow's mark, an indication that in their eyes he was both renegade and enemy.

"There's maybe a hundred of them, lacking paint but eager and ambitious," Mulroney went on. "They are on the far side of the big brook, plannin' a warm welcome for us when we cross over. Also, on that far bank there is a choice of gullies, leading back from the water. Whichever one we follow, up from the river, they will aim to be waiting for us."

It was jolting news, an abrupt end to the easy time they'd been having since leaving the lake country. Also, if Cherokees were lying in wait, that seemed to indicate that the Border Witch was no longer exerting a benevolent watch. Or were the proud Cherokee undaunted by such a threat?

Montana had planned to cross the river before halting for the night. It was a cardinal rule at a river never to put off till tomorrow what could be crowded into the present day. At sunset a stream might run softly, but sunrise could find it turbulent with flood, the result of a downpour farther upstream or along a tributary.

Now there was no choice except to camp, rather than risk the too eager welcome of the Indians. Yet they would be there the next day, or a week from then. They understood as well as Montana that he had to cross, and with no particular choice as to place. Should he move upstream or down, they would be ahead of them.

"There's mighty little sign of game hereabouts," Mulroney added. "In a day's riding by myself, I jumped one lone coyote, and it with a hungry look. So no doubt they are more than pleased to have a beef herd come their way."

Montana's own observations had been the same. There had been no sign of buffalo anywhere beyond the Red, and increasingly less of other game. This range had apparently been well hunted.

141

If there were half a hundred warriors on the far bank, that made two to their one. Striking from ambush, as they were coming out from the water, with his own crew hemmed and hampered by the deep narrow gulches running back from the river, such a force could be overwhelming.

"Let the herd water, then camp, as though that was the way we'd planned," Montana instructed. "Once it gets dark, we'll see about arranging a surprise party of our own."

Night would make it possible to slip across. At dawn, from higher ground, they might bushwhack the ambushers. The trouble was that such a plan might backfire, especially since they knew that Mulroney had gotten back with his report. The Cherokee would almost certainly have plans of their own.

Risk ran as strongly as the dark current of the river. A horse might thresh in treacherous waters as they neared the far shore, alerting the watchers, spoiling all chance at secrecy. A single mishap could be enough.

Clouds moved in with the sunset, a high cover shutting out the moon, blotting away the stars. That was luck, and Montana moved with it. He knew a moment of doubt, thinking what he might try if he were heading the war party. Suppose they decided to swim the river and overwhelm the camp? Doing that would be relatively easy and safe, especially if it was left unguarded.

But a choice had to be made, and Indians were traditionalists. Though excellent fighters, they generally followed their own rules of warfare slavishly. Why should they risk an attack, be forced to swim the river and perhaps run into strong opposition? If they waited, their victims must come to them. In any case, they preferred not to fight during the night, at least not until that drab hour, just short of dawn.

Montana divided his crew into two groups. One, led by Sam Henson, would head up-river for a couple of miles, then await his signal before crossing. An equal number, commanded by Mulroney, would go a similar distance downstream.

He would go straight across, with Curley, for another look. It was a feasible plan, at least in theory. The trouble with good plans was that a clever enemy might think along the same lines and be prepared. But war and battle were made up of such imponderables.

He was tightening the girth of his saddle when Cindy came out of the gloom. A thread of apprehension ran in her voice.

"Bill! You won't take any unnecessary chances?"

The oval of her white, upturned face was like a heart. Montana tried to put an easiness into his answer which he did not feel.

"I'm always careful of myself, Cindy."

"Are you, Bill?" Her laugh was uncertain. "Then isn't it strange I've heard so much the other way?"

"I'll sure aim to come back," he promised.

He scarcely felt the water as he slipped from the saddle and the current closed over him except for his head and shoulders. It was safer to swim beside his horse, keeping a low silhouette even in such uncertain light.

Curley was a short distance downstream. Montana's feet touched bottom as his horse stopped swimming. The current here ran swiftly, so strong he could scarcely stand against it, so that the shielding cayuse was welcome. The force of it had carried them quite a distance downstream, but they had allowed for that. The muted ripple of the water would cover such sounds as they made.

The night held a grayish quality, dark but not black. Higher light gave a luminous sheen to the clouds. Here, where cliffs rose sheerly from the water, the prospect was forbidding. The break of the gulch where they planned to ascend was a still deeper pocket of night.

Montana paused, feeling the shove of water

against his thighs, the chill touch of the night air above. Curley came alongside.

"You think they'll be waitin' for us?" he asked.

"Wouldn't you?" Montana countered.

Both of them had voiced their doubts. Montana was oppressed by a sudden fear, like the cold of the night wind. It might be the memory of Cindy which turned him squeamish, but that could be no more than a part of the reason. He'd felt the same sense of danger at other times, an eerie sense, hunch or instinct. It was a feeling he disliked but had come to trust. Every shadow had the semblance of a lurking warrior.

"Look. Off there." Curley's fingers bit into his arm, and his voice was tight.

There was a rising flicker against the night, gripping the nerves more tightly than Curley's fingers, the dread sense of the unknown. Had they been a little closer to the shore, the rising bluffs would have concealed it. Now, high up and distant, was a mounting glow, like a star grown suddenly luminous.

It was not quite that, nothing like anything which the lonely wasteland had known while baking through the heat of long summers or shivering under wintry blasts. Possibly the stalking dinosaur, eyes glazed by the fright of new and terrible events, had beheld something akin, as the young earth trembled and mountains spouted crimson rivers. But that had been far off and long ago.

Flame could lick red against the night, but this was a different flare, blood-red, soaring to the silent horizon, in an effect both strange and awesome.

Curley's fingers eased their grip. His voice breathed hoarsely in Montana's ear.

"They kind of remind me of Indian smokes – only these are sure the grandpappy of all such flares!"

16

Curley's voice was barely audible above the hurry and swish of the current; he was increasingly puzzled.

"See, there's another. Makes three of 'em. But I never saw anything like that before. They's like the fires of hell bustin' loose –"

That was a fairly apt description. Understanding was coming to Montana, a certainty with which relief mingled. The signals might be Indian style, but this time they were not Indian in origin. Someone who understood the talking smoke was behind these flares, and he needed only a single guess as to who.

That these high flares had been timed to convey a double meaning he did not doubt. Warriors had been waiting at the river bank, murderously intent. This had been the time and place for wiping out the drovers and capturing the herd.

So the signals were flaring across the night sky, for all to see and read.

"I don't quite make 'em out," Curley muttered, puzzled. "They seem to spell out smoke talk – talk of trouble."

"That's the way I read them, too," Montana agreed. The apprehension which had stretched his nerves was gone. "Those signals are meant for the Indians to read – but they aren't Indian!"

"You mean –?"

"My guess is that the white renegades are putting on this show. They want us to get as far as their country in good condition. Whether that's any favor or not is hard to tell. But they're warning the red men off. And I'll bet they're running like the devil after 'em."

"I'd be scootin' for other sections, too." Curley's voice held grim understanding. "They'll figure that thing is the Witch's doing – and it sure enough has the look of bad medicine. I can fair smell brimstone."

"Those are signal flares, burning a powder which was developed during the war," Montana explained. "It looks like devil's fire, sure enough."

The other Captain Abbott must have obtained a supply from somewhere, hoarding it against just such an occasion. Tonight it was being put to use. The message was a warning, and the crimson fires suggested unknown terrors. Superstitious warriors, beholding such a display for the first time, could hardly doubt that it was a portent of evil.

"Well, I guess what they're doing is intended as a favor for us." Curley shrugged. "And I won't say I'm not appreciative. But how we'll feel later on is something else."

"Yeah." Montana said nothing of his private knowledge, which was at least as disturbing as it was reassuring. Like the cattle, they were all being driven toward a showdown.

"Let's get on shore and have a look," he decided. "I doubt if there'll be anybody to hinder us now."

Yolande, called the Witch, had promised him her protection. Tonight she had made good that pledge. But he found himself shivering as he waded ashore.

The high cloud wrack was scattering, leaving a misty starlight which filtered into the canyon's depths. Beyond its reach, the shadows lay black and menacing.

The light revealed fresh sign just back from the water's edge, only minutes old. Warriors had prowled there even as they were setting out from the far shore, a reception committee who had clearly expected some such move on their part. But they were gone, and the pattern of prints in sand revealed how hasty had been their departure.

Twice as many men had been there as Mulroney had estimated. Even using all possible skill and wariness, it could have been grim.

"Waugh!" Curley expelled a pent-up breath as he read the sign. "Makes your hair stand on end, don't it? That was just a mite too close for my mammy's only son!"

In the distance, the crimson flares were fading, sinking against the night sky. There was no actual odor, but to an over-active imagination there seemed the scent of sulphur.

Tension marched with them. It was akin to a haze in the air, where actually there was nothing to see, nothing to touch. Taken as a whole, their luck had been more than good. There had been no stampedes, no losses at the rivers. Hindrances of any sort had been fewer than could be expected.

They were well up the trail, deep into the summer greenery of The Nations. Contrary to knowledge and expectation, it continued to be an empty land, at least outwardly. They marched through untroubled days, slept safely at night. That was the trouble.

"It's sure enough as though we're being protected from the usual run of Indians and renegades," Sam Henson fretted. "But who's doing it, and why? And for how long? I keep rememberin' that the tastier a trap's baited, the meaner it turns out to be."

Had any room for doubt existed in his mind, it was removed when Montana had a visitor. The kid found him, away from the herd, and he had clearly been waiting.

He lifted a hand in greeting, busying himself building a smoke, in no hurry to speak. Viewed by daylight, he was considerably older than Montana had supposed. Hair like bleached straw sprouted from beneath his shapeless hat.

Montana returned the salute but watched impassively. His silence jangled nerves already overly tight.

"What ails you?" the kid burst out angrily. "Are you plumb crazy, or just a fool? When a woman like Yolande loves you – do you have

150

to act like she don't exist, treat her like dirt under your feet? Other men'd give their right arm to be in your boots, but you – you just make her cry."

Had there been any doubt before, Montana was certain now. The kid was completely, hopelessly in love with the Border Witch. Accepting the reality of the situation, he was like a self-appointed watchdog. He was willing, even eager, to do anything to insure her happiness, whatever she might want.

"I've tried to treat her nice," Montana defended himself. "As to liking me, she hardly knows me. All I can be is one more man."

"No." The kid's head shake was positive. "There's been just two men in her life – and is it her fault if both of you have the same name and turn out to be the same sort? I happen to know that she left everything for Scott Abbott – following him to this country, just about worshipping the ground he rode across. And what did she get out of it? She found he was no good, as rotten as an apple at the bottom of the barrel –"

The kid's face twisted to match the bitterness in his voice. He went on wearily:

"After all she'd done for him, he treated her like dirt. She took it and came back for more. They call her the Border Witch, but he had a streak of the devil in him. Seemed like he *had* to act mean. He just about forced her to turn against him. Whatever he got then, he had it coming, and then some. And now, you –

"Oh, shoot," he added bitterly. "Maybe this ain't none of my business, but I'm making it mine. Here she's saving you from the Indians, offering you everything. Mister, get this straight! If you break her heart again, I'll kill you."

It was less a threat than a promise, as though such a duty had been laid upon him. With a final wild gesture, he swung away, and Montana watched him go, feeling a sense of hopelessness. If it had been only himself and his own happiness that were involved, he might have sacrificed them for others. But events had become so tangled that it went far beyond that.

He was not surprised when Yolande showed up again that night, riding silently out of the gloom, swinging her horse alongside his. He caught the faint fragrance of perfume such as ladies of the South had delighted in before the war – a forgotten luxury for most women.

Both horses halted, as if in common understanding. For a long moment there was the shuffling of hoofs, the impatient jingle of bridle bits, and the scent of bruised sage. Montana was acutely conscious of her nearness, of an exciting quality far stronger than perfume. Here was witchery if not witchcraft. Her voice breathed on a ripple of laughter.

"Have you no greeting for me, Bill? Do I make you tongue-tied? Or do I seem unwomanly, to seek you out, when it should be the other way around? But you have made no move – and here, in this land, which is my land –"

"You're certainly not unwomanly," he assured her, and again she laughed, swaying toward him. He felt mesmerized, caught and held by emotion more powerful than the noose of a lariat. It was his horse which broke the spell, not liking too close proximity with the other cayuse, swerving suddenly.

Mistaking the move for his own gesture, Yolande jerked back angrily. Even in the half-light, Montana saw an angry flush wash her cheeks. Her voice cracked like pond ice.

"You jerk away! Are you afraid of me – or are you a fool?"

Montana could have answered affirmatively and truthfully to both, so bemused had he been for the moment. Then suddenly he was his own man again. This woman was both beautiful and desirable, as soft as a kitten – but a kitten with claws.

She was altogether different from Cindy. The nature of that difference had been spelled out by the fiery signals which had leaped against the night sky. Shivering, he remembered the terror which had driven even so strong a man as Scott Abbott. Perhaps, as the kid insisted, Scott had it coming. But he had been pursued relentlessly, hounded to a nameless grave.

"My horse shied," Montana explained, and jerked it under control. But there was still distance between them, and her eyes narrowed angrily. "What do you expect?"

Clearly she did not believe him. "Have I not a right to expect more, after what I have done?" she demanded. Then her voice softened, grew suddenly appealing. "Have you no welcome for me, Bill?"

"Of course. I'm grateful for what you've done. I expect that you saved my life the other night – maybe saved all of us."

Her gesture was fiercely impatient. "Thanks and gratitude are not the same. Anyhow, I want neither – from you. I want more – much more, Bill."

Captain William Montana Abbott had known war and battle, the cold breath of terror and the hot sense of panic. Somehow those were emotions a man never quite lived down.

"Do you expect me to believe that so beautiful a woman as you can see anything to like in me?" he countered. "I'm not that conceited."

"Perhaps you should be. For it happens, Bill, that I do like you. Oh, is there no way to make you believe? This you may not credit, but you are the only man that I have ever cared for. It was not that I merely grew tired of Scott Abbott –" Her voice caught.

"If that had been all, it would not have mattered. I had married him in a moment of infatuation, and I sought to be loyal. That was not enough for him. He made me hate him – hate and despise him to the point where I could endure it no longer."

Montana believed her, feeling a growing uneasiness. Cold rage and blinding passion vied and mingled in her voice, and it was like winter wind. Then her tone changed again, becoming wheedling, almost pleading.

"You have changed, Bill – but I have not. I remember your arms, but you turn away from mine. Did those times mean nothing?"

"Maybe too much," he admitted unsteadily. "Do you think that any of this is easy?"

Curley was also riding night herd. His voice, low-pitched and cracked but singing a wild melody, warned of his approach.

"– On the soft summer air –"

Yolande gave an impatient exclamation, hesitated, then swung her horse away into the darkness. Curley came up, hailing cheerfully, keeping on without halting. Then Yolande was back, but again her mood had changed. Her voice was demanding, incisive.

"I think I understand. You are bemused by this other woman. You prefer her to me?"

A straightforward, honest answer might be best, but this was dangerous ground. Cynthia and her safety, as well as the fortunes of the others, were involved. Yolande was the leader of as wild a bunch as that lawless land had ever known. Still, she had admitted that she loved him, and he shrank from inflicting hurt.

"Miss Cartright is along because she owns part of the herd."

"Of course she owns it. That was not the question, but I have my answer. You are a poor liar, Mr. Abbott. It is her you love, then.

"So let us understand each other. If you really care for her, you can save not only her cattle but also her life. Do I need to remind you that death along the Border can come in many unpleasant forms?"

"I'm aware of that," Montana agreed. An anger equal to hers stirred the recklessness which was always near the surface. "Is that

156

the sort of love you have to offer – based on terror and threats?"

Her quirt lashed across his face before he could dodge or draw back. It was like a welt of flame, as her reaction was swift and bitter. Her arm lifted for a second stroke, then halted, and her eyes held a stricken look. But Montana's eyes were momentarily blinded, and agony fanned his rage.

"I think I like you better as a witch," he said tightly. "That's your true role, isn't it? As a woman, you've got just about every gift that nature could bestow – youth, beauty, charm. Probably you've had it hard in this rough land. But there's an old saying that you can catch more flies with honey than with vinegar. As far as I'm concerned, lady, I never did take kindly to threats."

Again, as the smarting subsided, he was startled at the change in her, the hurt and grief etched across her face. Here was a woman far beyond his understanding. It might be a trick of the light, or perhaps only a calculated wile, but there seemed to be tears glittering on her lashes.

"Oh, Bill," she sobbed. "I'm sorry – and so ashamed! You anger me because I love you so. Ah, if only we had met before – before so much had happened to divide us. But I

157

suppose we must face the fact that the river does not run uphill."

Silence fell between them. He sought helplessly for a reply, and she questioned him again, a breathless note in her voice.

"You will not forgive me? Must you be a knight-errant where this other woman is concerned – and also a fool? I thought that in the years of fighting you would have learned to be practical, not foolish."

"I guess I should have," Montana admitted. "But I've never been a practical man." He reflected grimly on the many times when that lack, or his streak of stubbornness, had cost him dearly. He had thrown away chances for promotion by ribbing superiors when he might have fawned; more than once he had angered men who had the power to make or break him.

It was still the same, except that the power had passed to a woman's hands, and he had not learned a lesson. Perhaps he had no right to be his own man, when that meant trifling with the safety of others, with their very lives.

His face still burned, but he was on the point of extending forgiveness, and asking it in turn, when her mood changed again. She had humbled herself, and it seemed that he scorned not only her plea but all that she offered. Her horse danced away, and for the first time her voice turned shrill.

"Have it as you will. You have just sealed the fate of this woman that you think you love – hers, and your own, and that of the others whom you might have benefited."

Her voice faltered.

"I'm sorry, Bill – but you had your chance. And I am not a saint – or even a witch, but a selfish woman.

"You should have held me, as you might have – held me as a hostage, if nothing else. Now it is too late – for everything. Had you made me your prisoner, I might have loved you for that. Now I hate you!"

17

Cindy was singing, bending above a pair of iron skillets, her cheeks like prairie roses from the heat of the cook fire, a strand of hair flying loosely below her left ear. Montana stood a moment, watching, before approaching. His breath quickened at the picture she made: he had forgotten the welt which still marked his own face. He took a step, and she looked up, her color waving like a flag. Then she came up from her heels with a rush.

"Bill – your face – what is it –"

He had decided on a story, which at least was partly true. To attempt to tell the whole truth would not only worry everyone needlessly, but entail explanations for which he had no liking.

"I ran into a renegade in the dark," he said. "He used his whip – and got away."

Cindy's fingers touched the still ugly welt questioningly; her eyes were big. The happiness had gone out of her voice.

"And I was just thinking that it was a glorious morning! I hadn't dreamed that this country could be so pretty. I'd always pictured it as wild and terrible – and of course it is!"

"There are a legion of lost souls who haunt it," he returned. "But it is a beautiful country. And some day there'll be homes here, and everything that goes with them."

But the pleasure had gone out of the day for him as well. Rolled in his blanket, he'd lain sleepless, pondering the mess he'd made of things. Had he any right to barter with the lives of this crew who followed his leadership, or to refuse to trade if by so doing he might get them through. Death, as Yolande had reminded him, came in unpleasant forms in

160

this country. Should he still ride, to seek her out and proffer his life for theirs?

He was still wondering when the herd lined out across a wide, green land. The day was as perfect an example of summer as a poet might picture. Then, abruptly, the prairie was empty no longer.

At first sight, Montana was not certain what it was that moved against the skyline, but his doubts were soon resolved as the vehicle approached. It was a wagon, with a high box above tall wheels, but lacking a canvas cover. Two horses snaked it along at a thundering gallop, running wildly, out of control. The course they followed would bring them athwart the van of the herd.

A man was on the wagon seat, but he seemed to have no control over the team. Terrified, the horses had taken the bits in their teeth and were running away. Montana and those nearest the wagon spurred to intercept them. Then he saw what it really was, and a sense of danger rushed like the onsweep of the wind.

The man was swaying and jouncing, more like a stuffed doll or a puppet than a creature of flesh and blood. The terror of the horses was partially explained as it became clear that the man no longer drove. The reins had been lost and were flapping about their legs, stepped upon, jerked and broken. They added to the panic, the horses sensing the lack of guidance.

Though in danger of losing his seat or being thrown out, the puppet still stayed in place. Then Montana saw why he remained, despite his helplessness. His hands were behind his back, tied at the wrists. A rope about his waist ran under the seat, holding him.

Here was treachery, as clever and ruthless as the tricks of a marauding wolverine. To interfere in what was happening was to risk the sort of death which drove the team, but it had to be attempted. The victim was the kid, but far more than his welfare was at stake. Unless halted, the runaways would panic the herd, causing a massive confusion in which the renegades would take control.

Montana had no doubt that the outlaws had started the team on their run. They would be waiting, just out of sight. To attempt a rescue would be to play their game, but it was that or leave the kid to a swift death if the wagon overturned, or a lingering one as the horses finally tired. He would remain bound and helpless, lost somewhere in the immensity of the prairie.

Forcing his horse alongside, a move which it resisted as if smelling the terror, Montana

162

grabbed at a rein close to the bit. His glance raked the contents of the wagon box.

At first sight everything seemed innocent and natural, almost too much so. It was as though the kid had been a farmer, returning from town with a load of supplies, covered loosely by a blanket. But at the edge of the blanket was a flicker of flame.

It was only a tiny spark, like the shimmer of a firefly in the vastness of night. But its meaning was only too clear, and understanding jolted him like the kick of a mule. Montana's reaching fingers missed their clutch at the bit, and his cayuse swerved away.

He was tempted to allow it to keep on widening the gap, to spur for a greater space between the wagon and himself. Beneath the blanket was a lethal trap which might erupt in thundering destruction at an instant. When it did, distance alone could save him from the fate which threatened the kid.

War was one thing, and he'd faced volleys of gunfire more than once, with men going down all around. But even in such a desperate fray, there was always the element of chance. Here there were no odds, only grim certainty.

The panic which drove the runaways had been communicated to his horse. He had to fight it around, closing the gap again, coming alongside. But now the long-range threat was as certain as the immediate one. The lives of his crew depended on it, their fate hanging on what he might do or fail to manage. If the wagon went up in a shattering blast, everyone from the San Saba would be finished along with it.

The very simplicity of the plan was the worst part. A high explosive, such as dynamite, could hardly be controlled in the swaying, jouncing wagon. Any jar might set it off, coming before it was intended, rendering the effect a dud.

But there were kegs of powder, their outlines showing under the blanket, and no such risk was entailed. Anchored, probably wired down to the floor of the wagon box, they could not roll. Only the flame, creeping along the fuse, could set off the charge.

Captain Scott Abbott had probably obtained the powder as a remnant of the war. This had been planned by someone familiar with the rate of burning fuse, matched to the speed of a wagon pulled by a galloping team. The flame was timed to reach the kegs as the wagon came up with the herd.

With several kegs of powder igniting, the giant blast would leave nothing of either the wagon or the team. Such cows as might be close at that fateful moment would become hamburger.

Such an explosion would throw the whole herd into panic, sending them out of control. The outlaws would have an easy victory over such scattered and disorganized crew members as might remain.

Most of them would be caught as the herd swung about, enveloped by the stampede. The wagons would be trapped in the same fashion. If they were lucky, they might be able to swing and run with the herd, possibly even survive the hazards of a trackless road. More likely, unable to turn, they would be pounded into the dust.

Survival of a few scattered members would leave the crewmen almost helpless, an easy prey. This would be the end of the drive.

Montana forced his horse back alongside the wagon. Kicking loose from the stirrups, he rose up, then flung himself at it. A miscalculation would send him under hoofs or wheels.

The wagon was there, as for an instant he hung poised. There was a painful smash as the side of the wagon box crashed against ribs and hip, spilling him inside in a rolling heap.

18

The wagon lurched wildly, the wheels on one side lifting over an upjutting boulder, throwing him against the opposite side of the box. He was as quickly bounced off again, lancing pain belying the airy ease of the movement.

His clutching fingers, seeking a hold, had snatched the blanket off the powder kegs, and he was right beside them. Grains of powder, a rusty black in appearance, had spilled from a small hole punched in the end of one keg. Through that opening, the now brief length of fuse vanished.

It must have been a long one when the driverless team had been set running. Now only a remnant remained, and to that the spark of flame clung doggedly, eating its way along like a hungry grasshopper.

Montana grabbed it and jerked. Another lurch of the wagon aided him. The fuse pulled loose, tearing out from the hole. More powder spilled as the opening was unplugged.

He flung the bit of fuse over the side, but there was no time to draw a full breath between sore rib cages. There was no more danger of a blast, but the still running team was nearing the herd. If they plunged headlong among the spooky steers, the stampede could still come off as planned, and just as disastrously.

His horse had kept running, and was now a considerable distance away, the flapping reins adding to its panic. Mounted on it, he would have had a good chance to stop the team. Now it would have to be done the hard way.

He clutched at the back of the seat, missing it as the wagon gave another lurch, narrowly avoiding smashing his face into it. Time was wasted holding to the side of the wagon box and pulling himself forward, but he dragged himself upright, then climbed across the seat. It too had been wired in place, to endure the jouncing of so wild a ride.

The kid sagged like a half-emptied sack of grain. There were no reins to reach or control the team. They had been left to flap about the rumps and hoofs, adding to the horses' fear as the leathers were trampled and broken.

The only chance to control the team was to climb down, onto the whiffletree, then work his way along the tongue of the wagon, between the horses. If he could reach a bit or get hold of a shortened rein, they might be slowed. But riding a bucking cayuse would be easy by comparison.

He glimpsed the slack-jawed face of the kid, too dazed even to show terror. But the eyes held a mute appeal. This seemed a poor sort of reward for the blind devotion which the kid had given the Border Witch.

Getting him loose while the runaway continued would hardly be a kindness, nor was there any time to waste. Grabbing the brake lever, Montana pulled it back, locking it in the last notch. The heavy wooden choks slammed, locking into place against the rims of the rear wheels, and the wagon gave a fresh lurch and grind. With this sudden drag, the headlong pace slowed, but not much. The madly running team were too terrified to be easily checked.

But a partial slow-down helped. Montana climbed down, holding to the front of the wagon box. He balanced on the swaying wood, getting set. A cautious approach would not work, and there was no time to spare.

The solid mass of the herd loomed ahead, brown backs, a sea of gleaming horns, baleful eyes which glared. The leaders had halted, staring suspiciously, pushed and shoved by the impatient crowding of the mass which until now had followed docilely. The sunlight reflected back from horns as from the drawn sabers of a battalion of cavalry. The herd was swinging to face this thundering menace

168

which rushed at them, ready to turn and plunge away at a fresh tangent.

Half-crouching, fingers touching the backs of the horses, Montana skittered ahead like a water bug, doing a gandy dance on the narrow, jerking wagon tongue. Muscles rippled under his hands as the plunging team strained to maintain their headlong pace. The odor of burning wood from the hard-set brakes added a new dimension of fear.

He missed a step, one leg plunging downward until the wagon tongue slammed against his crotch. Painfully Montana pulled back, reaching, fastening his fingers on the hame of the right-hand horse. Half-sprawling along its neck, he found the bridle rein and then took a hold with each hand on opposite sides. Knees braced against the hames, he reared back, twisting, increasing the pressure.

That was too much for the tiring animal. Running on nerve and terror alone, it was ready to quit, again to obey a guiding hand. It swerved to the drag on its mouth, dragging its mate with it. The wagon spun as sharply, and went over on its side in a splintering crash.

That halted them. The drag of half a ton, no longer on wheels, was too much. Montana was panting, gasping for breath, but the habit of command helped. He spoke calmly, and they were eager to obey. Heads lowered,

169

breaths wheezing, the pumping bellows raised small spurts of dust between their front legs.

The sudden silence was strange, uneasy. After the wild pound of hoofs and wheels, it had an almost chilling air of expectancy. The cattle still watched with uneasy suspicion, as ready as ever to break and run.

Montana slid to the ground, almost falling. He swayed dizzily, holding to a twisted trace until the spell passed. Then he made his way to where the kid lay, pinned down by the wagon seat and the side of the box. But they had jammed to form a sort of tunnel, saving him from much hurt. Once the rope which held him to the seat was loose, getting him out was fairly simple. The kid sat up dazedly, shaking his head, staring about as though this were a world he had never seen before.

"That's one ride I figured was going to end up in hell," he observed. "I thought I had a one-way ticket for sure."

Montana eyed the wreckage speculatively, the powder kegs and the milling, uneasy cattle. The attempt had come dangerously close to succeeding. Probably the renegades were still just at the edge of the horizon, awaiting the signal of the blast.

"They aimed to be rid of you, along with the rest of us." Montana nodded. "I don't know why they had it in for you, but it may be that we could make their scheme backfire." He indicated the powder kegs. "Blow that up in the faces of these critters, and they'd run – right back the way they came –"

The kid looked sick, but his head shake was violent. That he appreciated the possibilities of the suggestion was clear, but he was also appalled.

"No, no, you can't do that," he protested. "They've got it coming, sure – but it'd catch *her* along with the rest of them. She wouldn't have a chance –"

"You mean they're gathered just out of sight, over the hill? Or is that your camp?"

"They're there, and it's the camp," the kid conceded. "The hills sort of draw together, and the herd would be funneled to smash over everything and everybody." He was shaking with the vividness of what his imagination conjured.

"Then that's what they've got coming," Montana decided. "They set the trap, and now it's a question of who survives, they or us." He bent to tug at the kegs, to twist loose the wires which held them in place. "After the sort of reward you just received for being loyal, what's worrying you?"

"But you don't understand," the kid insisted, and crawled on his knees, breathing

171

heavily. "Sure the gang have got it coming, but not her. Yolande is a prisoner. They've locked her in one of the houses, and she wouldn't have a chance. The rest of them were determined to have the herd, and when she wouldn't go along with that, they turned against her –"

There was no doubting his earnestness, or that he was telling the truth. His loyalty to her explained why he had been tied to the wagon seat. He had backed her against the others, even though he realized the hopelessness of such a course.

The Border Witch had been the leader, but such leadership was tenuous with so lawless a rabble, as Scott Abbott had discovered. She, too, had gambled once too often, for too high stakes –

If the kid's devotion was blind, Yolande's was no less faithful. That he was the reason, the object, rocked Montana back on his heels. The love of a woman – or a man, as the kid had shown – could be beyond understanding. Not all emotions on the border were evil or savage.

One part of his mind understood and accepted this. The other side battled against a tame surrender, against throwing away what might be their best chance for victory and survival.

"Somebody's crazy," Montana said grimly, "likely you and me both. What does she know of loyalty? Look what she did to Scott –"

"He was a devil, and he got just what he deserved," the kid panted. "I tell you she's a good woman, only she's never had a chance. I guess she thought a lot of him, for he sure turned her head to start with. She left everything behind for him, coming here, figuring that he loved her. She got here, only to find that he had another woman, a squaw, and that she was to be just another squaw, not even number one –"

The kid's head shake was more sorrowful than vindictive. Montana studied him with growing respect. Such loyalty was revealing.

"Abbott soon found out what a mistake he'd made. She's not a woman to be treated like a toy or a dog. You were around to see what happened to him; he had it coming. And now she's gambled everything for you –"

Montana felt suddenly drained and tired. The last thing he'd ever wanted or intended was to find himself in the middle of such a situation; but like the kid, here he was. And, again like him, he could end up taking a one-way ride to ruin.

While they talked, the moment for striking back had passed. The cattle, high-strung only moments before, were starting to drift away,

173

to graze. There had been no blast as a signal, and by now the outlaws would have a pretty good understanding of the situation. The chance of a counter-attack was lost.

Had there been any doubt, it was removed as a horseman rode into sight, gesturing with an upraised hand. The kid eyed him warily.

"That's Hatfield," he explained. "He led the revolt against Yolande. Whatever he has in mind, it'll be stinkin' mean!"

19

Hatfield's lips drew back in what was intended for a grin, but more nearly resembled a snarl. As raw-boned as a starving wolf, he belonged in a lobo pack.

The trail crew, who had been widely scattered, were starting to come, but were still too distant to take any part in the action. Hatfield's eyes darted nervously.

"So you're Abbott Number Two – which makes you a second-class man," he observed, and cackled shrilly at his own wit. "I might shoot you down, as happened to him – or have others do it." He waved a careless hand toward other figures who had come into sight,

174

sitting their horses, rifles held at the ready. "That's a temptation, but I'll forgo it, for I promised the boys a bit of sport – always supposing, of course, that you're willing to cooperate." Again he cackled mockingly.

Centuries had rolled before the sun since the Romans had brought the circus to a high degree of popularity, making a brutal spectacle of human slaughter. Now it was as though time stood still. These outcasts of the Border had established a reputation for similarly bizarre entertainment. They gave a careless allegiance to leaders who could furnish it to them, and the more savage and unpredictable, the better.

"What's your idea of cooperation?" Montana countered. "A fight, man to man, winner take all?"

Hatfield's cackle was intended to express contempt, but it seemed more a cloak for uncertainty.

"You're close, mister. Only you'll fight another man. If you win – I say *if* – then you can go on with your herd. But if you lose –" His shrug was mocking.

The kid had struggled to his feet. He was spent and sick, and he spoke hoarsely.

"Don't trust anything he says, Montana. Even if you should be lucky, he wouldn't keep his word."

Hatfield swung toward him, snarling, but checked as Montana put himself between them.

"Easy," he warned. "He's had it rough, playing his part in your show. Now we'll leave him out of it."

Hatfield glared; then his gaze shifted nervously. "Yes," he agreed. "He don't count."

This would be playing the outlaw's game, where there were no rules. Montana had no doubt that the kid was telling the truth. But it was not a matter of choice. Also, Yolande was in trouble on his account. Her last words to him had been that she hated him, but clearly that had not been so. She was a woman, with a woman's unpredictability, but also a woman's loyalty.

"Bring on your man," he invited. "I'll fight him, winner take all. And Mrs. Abbott is a part of the deal. She's to be free to go or do as she pleases."

"You think you stand a chance, eh?" The cackle was grating on Montana's nerves. "Sure, we won't argue that point."

As they talked, the trail crew had been coming up, warily suspicious as they understood what was happening. Additional renegades made a matching show of force. The two groups had halted just beyond easy revolver shot, but within easy rifle range.

The cattle had gone back to grazing, their panic subsiding. Sam Henson shook his head dubiously.

"I don't like this, Montana," he protested, then added softly, "And we won't be bound by any sort of deal, if the going gets rough. They wouldn't live up to their part."

"I've made no promises on your account," Montana returned. But the simple mathematics of the situation were beyond argument. They were heavily outnumbered, and it would be a slaughter should he refuse.

"Since you're agreeable, let's not keep folks waiting," Hatfield gibed, and swung his horse, leading the way. Montana followed, the kid stumbling in his wake. The crew moved, maintaining the same distance from the outlaws, both groups alert, but respecting a temporary truce.

From the crest, a long valley opened up, narrowing sharply about half a mile ahead. There, a huddle of buildings marked the headquarters of the Border wolves. They had some semblance to ranch buildings, but possessed the impermanence of a camp.

A considerable remuda of cayuses watched their approach from a pole corral, thrusting necks eagerly over the top stringer. One nickered in welcome. Four wagons were

177

drawn up before a squat barn, two with canvas covers. The canvas sagged disconsolately, the ribs of the hoops showing like skeletons. A plow was still wired and roped to the side of one wagon, its share dull with rust.

Tools and farm equipment were scattered about, booty from looted wagon trains. Apparently they had been lured off course, then attacked, perhaps being fooled into believing that they were approaching an honest settlement. Montana could picture the pleasure of immigrants upon sighting such a haven in the center of so wide a land – a surprise with betrayal at the end.

Hatfield gave another cackle of laughter.

"Welcome to Rebel's Ranch, Abbott – called, upon occasion, Traveler's Treat! And don't think they don't!"

This renegade village was about as Montana had expected, a sorry headquarters. Even to the renegades it must appear a dismal haven, with the long-range prospects even worse than the uncertain present. Under such conditions, the savagery with which they welcomed a show, any break in the monotony, was understandable.

The accumulated bitterness of hopelessness and frustration was ingrained on nearly every face. These men had once held high hopes, dreamed dreams, and this was the nightmare awakening. Not only were they failures in society, but the worst part was their knowledge of their failure, along with a lack of hope. Once they had been free men; now they were prisoners, of their own making.

No time was lost. The two factions were lining up as spectators, keeping apart, not far from the edge of the camp. Outnumbering the Texans by at least two to one, the outlaws eyed Hatfield expectantly.

"Where's Prine?" Hatfield demanded irritably. "Step out, man. Or ain't you proud to be doing the honors for our side?"

There was a momentary hesitation. Then a tall man, barrel-like in build and girth, emerged reluctantly from the gather. He clearly was not overjoyed at being selected to oppose Montana.

"Why pick on me?" he demanded sullenly.

"Why not?" Hatfield countered. "You've made your brag, often enough, about how good a man you are. And it was your idea to send that team running with those kegs of powder. It was a scheme that couldn't help but work – to listen to you. Well, you know the rule. When somebody makes a bad mistake, he gets a chance to pay for it."

Prine shrugged heavy shoulders dejectedly. This was clearly an established rule among the renegades. No mercy was shown for mistakes.

Hatfield dismounted, glaring at Prine until he shrugged an acceptance. Then Hatfield turned to Montana.

"You two look to be pretty well matched in size, so this should be a good fight. It'll be fair, no odds either way. Hold out your hand – your left hand."

There was a tingling at the short hairs of Montana's scalp, a sense of unreality. The others, knowing what was coming, were waiting avidly. Having no choice, Prine would fight desperately for his life. Nothing less hinged on the outcome.

A few steps to one side, the grass grew long and tangled. Hatfield pulled a hand from a capacious coat pocket, and something gleamed in his grasp. He moved fast, there was a click, and Montana felt the coldness of steel about his wrist. One link of a handcuff had been snapped shut.

"This lil' toy is just to make sure of fair play between the two of you," Hatfield explained, and cackled gleefully. "And it makes sure that neither of you can quit or run out before the game's finished. You, too, Prine."

They would be given knives now, and this was to be a struggle to the death. One of them, with luck, might survive. Even the luck would be a chancy thing. If he ended up badly injured, still shackled to a dead man, among a crew eager for the spilling of more blood –

Prine submitted sullenly, and the other link of the handcuff was snapped on his left wrist. There was a stifled ejaculation from one of the big wagons which had drawn up. Montana knew that Cindy had cried out.

"Oh, this is horrible – monstrous!" Her voice was a gasp.

" 'Tain't nothin' pretty, for a fact," Mandy returned grimly. "But let's us not be forgettin' who's fightin', missy!"

Another man approached, carrying a pair of knives which appeared to be identical. They were long-bladed, murderous weapons, ground to a keen edge. Montana swung on Hatfield.

"Where's Mrs. Abbott? You trying to renege on me?"

Hatfield looked sullen, but gave an order. "Since he wants her to see him die, bring her out," he shrilled.

That created a brief diversion, a few additional moments before he and Prine would do their best to murder each other.

Yolande approached, between two guards. Apparently she had not wanted to be a

181

spectator. She sank onto a stool which someone provided.

Silence fell, as everyone waited expectantly. What might happen at the end could be savage and explosive, but the fight would come first.

"Take your positions," Hatfield ordered, pointing to the patch of tall grass. "Step careful, gents. When you're ready, you'll be given your knives."

Looking more closely, Montana paled. Hand to hand and blade to blade was bad enough, but this was a variation; an unchancy dividend, to earn loyalty to a leader who would provide such sport.

Partly concealed among the ankle-high grass were steel traps – at least a dozen, possibly a score. They were set and ready, arranged in an irregular pattern. With double springs compressed, the wide jaws gaped, ready to leap and close at a single misstep.

20

The traps were probably booty from some raid on a wagon train, useful to a mountain man or a settler, but of no use to the outlaws except for such a show. They were massive instruments, as was required for the intended game. The heavy jaws would snap shut, closing high on the leg of a captive. Once caught, even a grizzly bear would be helpless in such an embrace.

From where the chuck wagon had pulled up, it was too far for Cindy to see what the grass hid, though by now she had probably guessed. Yolande, of course, knew. Witch she might be termed, but her disinclination to watch the show was understandable.

Here were two women, each of whom had tried to help him. One, he suspected, loved his brother, and Yolande had admitted that she loved him. What she had tried to do for him had brought her to her present fall from power.

So their fate, like his own, hinged largely on what he might be able to do now. Like Prine, he had no choice. But this was more than he'd bargained for.

Enough space had been left between the traps for a man to walk, given time to pick and choose each step. But in the excitement of a life-and-death struggle, hurried, distracted by a slashing or murderously driven knife, a misstep, sooner or later, was inevitable.

Prine moved carefully to the middle of the thicket. Montana could see the sweat popping on his face and neck as he tried to watch his step while keeping his attention on his opponent. They had each been handed a knife; then the others drew back.

Prine gave a sudden lunge with a shoulder, hoping to catch him off guard, to send him stumbling. Montana met the shove with a counter-thrust of elbow and shoulder, but the barrel-like figure was swift to recover, standing like a post.

Prine had relied on surprise, hoping that the bear traps would make the necessary difference. Such action left him momentarily exposed to a counter-thrust, but Montana deliberately held back his counter-stroke. Victory here could be hollow, only a prelude to worse things. He caught the flicker of doubt in Prine's eyes as he sensed the withholding, but how the outlaw might react there was no way of knowing.

There would be no rounds in this contest, no rules. The links of the handcuff tensed on his wrist, and against them Montana made a twisting lunge. Prine's counter-effort jerked his arm a fraction to the side, spoiling both tries.

This time Prine was first to recover, twisting in a dervish effort, trying to lunge and stab. The knife blades clashed, sparks glinting. The knife in Montana's hand was all but torn from his grasp, and blood gushed as the edge grazed his wrist. A shout went up from the watchers.

The sensation of pain quickened his perceptions. Montana smashed down with the handle of his knife, catching Prine across the back of the hand. Agony twisted the outlaw's face, but he clung fast to his weapon.

Prine's lips snarled back from his teeth as they eyed each other. The opposing lines of spectators were gradually pressing closer, almost as near as the maze of traps permitted. Hatfield was in the forefront.

Prine gave a jerk of arm and body, using the linked handcuffs, hoping again to make Montana stumble. His blade, part of the same effort, struck like a rattler.

Sparks spattered off gouging steel, and they were close-locked, struggling desperately. The jaws of a trap snapped, leaping to released tension. Montana sensed that his boot had brushed the pan, triggering it. His legs jerked in response, barely ahead of the jaws.

A widening puddle of crimson stained Prine's left cheek. Abruptly changing his tactics, the outlaw grabbed Montana's knife wrist, at the same time pointing his blade toward Montana's throat. A shout erupted from the watchers, where there had been only strained silence. They were eager for blood.

The power of the barrel-like figure was able to make itself felt now, showing in a ridge of muscle along humping back and shoulders, like a grizzly's. Montana's arms were heavy with the effort to hold; they felt about to crack, to give way. The only recourse, other than to await the inevitable, was to risk the traps, taking a blind chance. It would involve both of them equally. Montana lunged, twisting and heaving.

The crest of the blade twisted past his shoulder as he gave ground, and Prine's mouth opened, bawling like a wounded steer. He tried a frantic counter-stroke, but was checked by the relentless jerk of the handcuffs, then the snap and crunch of heavy steel snapping shut. His knife spilled groundward.

Now was Montana's chance to drive home his own thrust, but he checked the stroke. More even than in the games of the ancient Romans, here no mercy would be shown even for the victor.

His knife might be put to better use.

Instinctively, as the big trap sprung and its jaws found a hold, every eye had shifted to Prine and his bad luck. In that instant when attention was elsewhere, Montana flung his knife at the nearest onlooker, a redheaded man whose whiskers stood out like a red flag.

He was leaning forward, mouth partly open, his eyes glittering like those of a fox. Taken by surprise, he still managed to jerk away from the hurtling blade, but stumbled with the effort, going to his knees. Again, for an instant, everyone's attention was drawn.

Linked wrist to wrist with Prine, Montana was handicapped, but for the moment the renegade was concerned only with the bone-crushing jaws about his ankle. Bending down, Montana snatched another trap, seizing a compressed spring with his free hand. The trigger had been set lightly, trembling of its own weight as the trap was moved.

Holding the menacing jaws before him, Montana plunged ahead, jerking Prine helplessly in his wake. More traps were springing, jumping behind them, the snapping jaws clicking angrily as the dragging chains tangled and dislodged still others. Risking a misstep, Montana reached the rim of the thicket where Hatfield was standing, frozen momentarily in his tracks by the speed of the unexpected.

Hatfield was like a sleepwalker, starting back in terror. It was only for an instant, but that was long enough as Montana lifted the trap and Prine's linked arm, to bring the gaping jaws suspended above Hatfield's head.

Should they snap, the released springs would lash the steel about his throat or chin.

"Hold steady, Hatfield," Montana warned. "Prine, take it easy. One wrong move on anybody's part," he added, "and I'll be trapping skunks! If you try to jerk or dodge, you'll be too late, Hatfield."

Hatfield's heavy face had gone as flabby as the underside of a fish. Prine's was equally bloodless, from the agony caused by the jaws around his ankle.

A man at the rim of the circle shuffled his feet, but the others were careful to avoid even such uneasy movement. Anyone who chose might use a gun, and a single well-placed shot could kill Montana. But such a shot would set off a general conflict, and it would be of no help to Hatfield. The trap would have sprung.

"This trap's heavy," Montana observed, and his tone was conversational, but with a threat like the steel. "I can't hold it steady very long, my friend. So since you've got the key, you'd best unlock these handcuffs and ease the strain."

Hatfield's eyes rolled, showing whites like those of a spooky cayuse. He had seized power here, and further triumph had been a heady draught. But the throttling noose of

188

the trap's jaws sent ice coursing in his veins. He obeyed, though his hand was shaking so that he could hardly fit the key and release the steel link.

As the handcuff dropped away, Montana moved fast. In a single sweeping gesture he tossed the trap to the side and snatched the revolver from Hatfield's holster. The trap struck and snapped as if in frustration, but by then the muzzle of the outlaw's gun was nudging hard against his own ribs.

"Let's everybody take it easy," Montana added, and a grin lifted the tips of his mustache. "You made a nice try, Hatfield, but it didn't work. Now we'll be moving along with our herd – and you'll go with us for a while, too. And of course the lady will come with us, if she so desires."

He owed that much to Yolande. Her life was as much at stake as his. What further troubles might erupt from such a company on the trail he tried not to think about. With Cindy and Yolande both in the same camp – he would be more than ever in the middle. But Yolande, the Border Witch, was also a great lady, and he owed her a debt.

Hatfield tensed momentarily once the threat of the trap was removed, but the gun was equally potent. He relaxed, and the crisis was past.

Yolande came slowly to her feet, for once uncertain. Then she managed a smile as one of Montana's crew drew alongside with a saddled horse, stepping down to hold it for her.

"If you'd care to ride, ma'am, this is a good hawss," he offered gallantly.

"Why, thanks, it is most kind of you," she returned, and drew herself up and into the saddle. Observing her with sudden tenseness, Montana saw that her easy grace was gone, the effort of mounting all that she could manage. But a smile was still on her lips as she grasped the reins, then swung the horse with a sudden frantic touch of the reins and a coaxing voice. In that same instant the blast of a gun broke like a snarl against the silence.

21

The shooting was over and ended almost as suddenly as it had erupted, once the explosive savagery of the renegade Border had vented itself. Three men were on the ground, dead in as many seconds. Yolande, the uncertain smile gone from her face, was swaying, falling from the saddle, as Montana jumped and caught and eased her down, holding her in his arms. The beat of her heart seemed to falter, then race against his own. Her pulsing blood was soaking through her dress, staining his shirt to a matching crimson.

It had been a vengeful, desperate try, and the bullet had been intended for him. She had seen the gunman's intent and swung her horse, putting herself in the way, taking the slug from the six-gun. That the kid, watchful as well, had managed to grab a gun and down the killer in turn was an anticlimax, as was the fact that in his frenzy he had then turned the gun on Hatfield, while another man had leveled on him.

It was an ending which would probably have pleased the kid, had there been any chance to plan it. He had avenged his lady, and died with her.

Cindy was down from the chuck wagon, beside Montana, helping as he eased Yolande to the ground. Her eyes were wide with compassion as she brushed back the hair from Yolande's face, so that her uncertain gaze could find what it sought. Again, this time in sheer gallantry, Yolande's smile touched her lips.

"You love him, too," she murmured. "So take him, my dear. I'm astonished at myself," she added, and her voice was a sighing breath, so that Montana and Cindy were forced to bend low to hear her. "I never expected to be generous in such a fashion."

Her breath slowed, her eyelids drooping wearily. Then they came open, almost on a questioning note.

"But then – love and death have both been strangers to me – until now –"

Her head turned slightly, her eyes seeking Montana's. In them was agony and appeal.

"If you would kiss me, Montana – just once –"

He bent quickly, choking, and her lips moved, responsive to his own. Then they grew still, and the smile on her face was fixed and peaceful as he straightened. He caught Cindy's glance, and on her face was a blending of compassion and dismay.

"Poor lost lady," he muttered. "Poor, lonely little girl."

"She was a lady," Cindy admitted. "And she loved you. But she didn't understand –"

"I know," Montana admitted. "And that made her twice as gallant."

Cynthia touched the still cheek gently, then loosened a row of buttons to disclose the newly stained bandage beneath – a bandage which confirmed Montana's earlier guess.

"She had been shot," she said. "That's how Hatfield managed to take over. She was so badly hurt that she should not have moved – but she came out and watched, and proved herself still the leader."

By now understanding was spreading, and anger among the outlaws was like a rising wind. All their rage was directed against the dead usurper. There were standards even here, a rough but ready code which Hatfield had violated. At the last, he'd been luckier than he knew. Death had placed him beyond their reach.

The Missouri frontier was like the breaking of sun across the land after a night of storm. The market was there, with buyers waiting and eager. That a blighted strip of rangeland should or could divide a country seemed part of a nightmarish dream, from which they had finally awakened.

But that renegade Border was real, and the fact that they had crossed it from south to north was no guarantee they would be able to do so again, reversing their course. Missouri was actually the halfway mark, no more. With knowledge as a guide, Montana lifted his gaze to the west, then contemplated the return journey bleakly.

He'd headed for Texas and Tom Abbott, and having seen Tom, he was fiddle-footed again, itching to get back to Montana. But a job couldn't be shucked off, half-done.

He had paid off a few of the men, and all had received some wages. But the bulk of the proceeds, the gold on which hinged the success or failure of the drive, remained to be gotten back to Texas, to flow like a fresh infusion of rich blood along the San Saba.

There had been a tacit truce, inspired by fear and hate and respect, all curiously blended. But that was a part of the past, and memories were short. The renegades, reorganized and with new, uncommitted leadership, would be waiting for them to try and make it back, knowing that they would be bringing gold.

Trailing north to Missouri, they had had a lot of luck. Going back would be equally dangerous, especially because of Cindy. Montana knew only too well how failure could fester, becoming an itch, a goad. The small marker above a lonely grave, at which both sides had marked a truce and stood bareheaded in the rain, would not be a talisman.

Meditatively, Montana gave a twist to his mustache, then swung at a hail. The shout rose genially above the tramp and jingle of a sound which he knew well, that of cavalry horses, a file of mounted men in blue.

The sight of them was astonishing, though no more so than the sight of the captain who rode at their head. It was three days since he'd paid Mulroney off, and he'd supposed him long gone to greener pastures. Yet here he was, saluting smartly, then dismounting and extending a hand in greeting. His smile was quizzical beneath the jaunty sweep of his mustache.

"Sure, and I don't suppose that seeing me this way is any great surprise to you, Montana," Mulroney observed. "I was a Yankee; you might almost call me a carpetbagger. Having come to think of myself as a Texan, I covet a spread on the San Saba – perhaps the one that Watson had preempted, adjoining that of your brother.

"And of course that's not all. You'll have guessed, perhaps, that I was under orders to journey north from there and see for myself the conditions between. Sure, and it was a piece of luck that you took me under your wing. We both know what we found – intolerable conditions, which cannot be permitted to continue. I have my command here, with orders to go through again to Texas, to open the trail a bit wider. It is my hope that you and the others whom I am honored to count as friends will journey with us." He bowed sweepingly.

"I'll not be so brash as to suggest that we take you under our wing, Captain Abbott. Let it be a joining of forces, fighting men all. For my part, I'll feel safer with the same crew – and to insure that no harm comes to Cindy, who has done me the honor to agree to change her name to mine, once we are again in Texas –"

Cindy was coming from a store, coloring at the sight of Mulroney, then advancing to stand beside him. Montana was struck by surprise, reflecting again that women always had the power to bewilder as well as charm. But his congratulations were hearty, more so as he looked again toward the sweep of the broad Missouri. The sun was suddenly warm in a blue sky.

"It's a load you take not only off my mind but off my feet, Captain," he assured Mulroney. "May you have a fair, safe journey. But you have no more need of me. There's a packet about to head up-river for Benton and Montana, and I'll be on her, riding like a gentleman. And what could be finer?"